Books by Anna Lee

Sexy Snax

The Broken Road

Single Titles

His Soldier

His Soldier

ISBN # 978-1-78651-906-1

©Copyright Anna Lee 2016

Cover Art by Posh Gosh ©Copyright 2016

Interior text design by Claire Siemaszkiewicz

Pride Publishing

Published in 2016 by Pride Publishing, Newland House, The Point, Weaver Road, Lincoln, LN6 3QN, United Kingdom.

Printed in Great Britain by Clays Ltd, St Ives plc
1

HIS SOLDIER

ANNA LEE

Dedication

To all those who serve our country, thank you.
To my family, I love you all.
To Sassy, my little diva.
And last but certainly not least, thanks to my editor, Sue,
for all her encouragement and hard work.

Chapter One

Spring Lake, North Carolina

'Baby, they showed up at the house, I just knew... Oh God, Dax, my boy... They said it was an IED... Can you drive? Dean? Please, I need you, son... You're all I have left...'

He had just gotten home from work — a teacher's meeting had run late. He hadn't even had a chance to put his book bag down before his phone had rung. He'd answered then dropped the bag, his keys and thrown his phone. Dean left his house, barely remembering to shut the door. He ran all the time, just not in pants, a button-up shirt, and tie. He got a few odd and concerned stares but he ignored everyone. His feet hit the pavement and he didn't even think about where he was going. His only thought was maybe if he kept running he could escape the pain and the new hole in his chest. Try as he might to ignore it, Beth's voice rang in his head.

'Baby, they showed up at the house, I just knew... Oh God, Dax... They said it was an IED... Can you drive? Dean? Please, I need you, son... You're all I have left...'

Tears streamed down his face as he kept going until he somehow wound up in the park. Out of breath, and unable to fight it, he leaned against an old oak tree, gasping, bent over at the waist. When he caught his breath, forcing air in and out again, he thought about continuing the run until he noticed he was at the tree that held so many memories. He looked up, recalling the summer they had both broken their arms when they were eight. Then at eleven they had tried to build a fort but Parks and Rec made them take it down,

5

though Dax had sure fought it. And at sixteen... Well, he'd found out who his true family and friends were, with Dax proving he was the brother Dean had always wanted.

Even though it was fifteen years ago, he remembered that day as if he was sixteen all over again.

He dropped his sleeping bag and backpack next to the old oak. After sinking down into the soft grass, he wrapped his arms around his knees and tried not to cry. His whole body hurt but that was nothing compared to his dad disowning him. For being who he was and finally admitting it. He was gay. And now he was homeless. What was he going to do?

He was so tired and sore that he must have dozed off or blacked out. He wasn't sure. He was startled to hear his name. "Dean? Buddy?" Dax knelt beside him. "I thought that was you."

Dean looked up, swiping at his runny nose. "Dax..." He knew his face was a wreck — busted lip, black eye, a cut above his left temple. He was pretty sure he had a cracked rib and maybe even a broken wrist. The horror of it showed on Dax's face but was quickly replaced with anger.

"Who the hell did this to you? I'll kick their asses!" Dax growled, searching around as if Dean's attackers were nearby. Dean didn't doubt, if it had been a bully, that Dax could take them. Whereas he was scrawny and still trying to build muscle, Dax was strong and had a broad-shouldered frame that showed off his athletic prowess. They were opposites — Dean had black hair and green eyes, Dax blond hair and blue eyes. But they had grown up together, thick as thieves, and remained friends even in high school. No one picked on him for being nerdy because Dax was so popular.

"You can't go after my old man."

"He hit you? Why the heck would he do that? You never get in trouble without me."

Dean was so scared. He'd already lost his family. If he told Dax would he hit him too? Would he walk away and leave him all alone? Dean wasn't sure he wanted to live if that happened. What was the point if no one cared? "Because... I'm gay," he whispered.

Dax seemed shocked for a moment. "You are?"

6

"Yeah, my dad beat my ass when I admitted it."

"Your dad is an ass, why did you tell him?"

"'Cause Mom caught me kissing Stevie," Dean confessed, and Dax's eyes widened. "She made me tell my dad then just watched as he hit me over and over. When I got up he threw me out in the yard. I snuck back in and got some of my stuff but I… I don't have anywhere to go, Dax. They hate me." He let out a strangled sob then added, "Do you hate me too?"

"For being gay? No, why would I? You're still my best friend." Dax paused, then, to Dean's surprise, pulled him in for a quick hug. It was a brief comfort that lifted a weight from his shoulders. "Don't cry. We'll fix this. You can stay with me."

"What if your mom doesn't like me being gay?"

"My Uncle Eric is gay. No big deal."

Dean couldn't believe it, but relief washed through him. Dax's family wouldn't care about him being gay — maybe he wouldn't have to live on the streets. He could get a job or something, pay them to stay there. Just until college. He was going to get a scholarship and study. "How come you never told me that?"

Dax shrugged. "You've never talked about your aunt who lives in Florida or your uncle in Nebraska. You know family stuff is boring. Anyway, he lives in San Diego with his husband and I've visited him a few times. He's cool. We'd probably visit more if we could afford it. Mom talks to him every day, though."

"Oh…" Dean wiped his eyes. "I'm glad you don't hate me."

"I hate your old man. What kind of crap is that? You're his kid, and your mom. Man, my mom is gonna flip." Dax whistled. "She'll let them have it. I bet she could get them to understand. She got my grandpa to come around."

Dean shook his head. "I don't want to go back. They won't ever understand. I can't live there knowing they think I'm wrong. And what if he hurts me again?"

"There's nothing wrong with you." Dax looked like he wanted to hit Dean upside the head for saying it. "I'll take on anyone who says there is, even your old man. We're blood brothers, right?"

A tiny smile twitched Dean's lips. "Right."

Dax stood and held out a hand. "C'mon, I bet you're hungry."

He grinned. "Man, you know what this means?"

"What?"

"More chicks for me!" Dax chuckled as Dean punched his arm. "What? I was just trying to get you to laugh."

Dean shook his head. "Ha ha." He grabbed his backpack and Dax took the sleeping bag. "Thanks, Dax."

Dax slung his arm around his shoulder. "Any time, little bro."

They walked to Dax's house slowly — Dean was in a fair amount of pain and it hurt to even breathe too deeply. When they reached the one-story bungalow, Dean paused on the steps, wrapping his arms around himself.

"What's up?" Dax asked.

"What if your mom tries to make me go home? Or Social Services comes and takes me away?" Tears prickled his eyes. He swiped at them. "I don't want to go anywhere."

"Hey, I meant what I said." Dax laid a gentle hand on his shoulder, not his usual roughness. "I promise, I'll do whatever I got to so you can stay here, 'kay?"

Dean nodded then hugged Dax again. He just wanted to feel safe. And he did with his brother.

"Dax!" his mom called out as she stepped onto the front porch. "Dean, what in the heavens!" She rushed to him and drew him into an embrace. He held on, burying his face in her shoulder as his body shook. "What happened, sweetheart? Dax, baby, who did this?"

Dax growled. "His old man beat on him 'cause he's gay."

Dax never did sugarcoat anything. Dean waited for Mama Beth's reaction. He called her that as she was like the mom he'd always wanted with hugs, cookies and nurturing. He knew she wouldn't send him away but he was still scared. After what his dad did, it felt like he wasn't on solid ground. "Please, can I stay with you? Please?" He added in a rush, "I'll do chores, get good grades, make you proud, I promise. Just please, I feel safe here, and I can't go back or go to some foster home."

"Shh." Mama Beth soothed him, pressing a kiss to the top of his head. "Of course you can stay, you know I'm a foster mom. We can make sure I get custody of you so no one hurts you again."

She rubbed his back, and he winced. "I think we need to take you to the hospital."

"No, I hate hospitals!"

She pulled back and gently cupped his face. "Tough, you need to get checked out. I'm not having you in this much pain. Does anything feel broken?"

"Ribs, maybe," Dean admitted. "My wrist, too."

She cradled it in her hands and inspected it. The wrist was swollen and didn't bend so well.

"Ouch."

"I'm sorry, we definitely have to see a doctor. It'll be okay, though." She locked gazes with him. "We need to have them report this, I'm not letting that idjit get away with it. No one should ever hurt their children. It's inexcusable and unforgivable."

Dean dropped his head. "I'm a sinner, that's what they said. That God wanted them to punish me."

"They're wrong, baby," Mama Beth said. "They're sinning against Jesus' commandment to love everyone as he and God do."

Dax growled again and headed toward the door. "I'm getting Daddy's shotgun and making that SOB pay."

"Daxson Chase Anders, you will do no such thing," his mom ordered. "Even if I want to as well. We'll have them answer for this, just let me take care of it."

"Okay, Mama." Dax rejoined them. "But if he shows up here all bets are off."

Dean looked between them both and almost chuckled. It meant a lot that they wanted to protect him. Dax was always fighting for him, and he was lucky to have them both. "He won't. They're glad I'm gone."

"Their loss. You belong here anyway," Dax said with a grin. "You always fit better here."

"It's true, I've always had two sons." Mama Beth kissed his forehead. "I love you, Dean. Just the way you are. It don't matter one bit that you're gay — you're still family and always will be."

"Mama's right."

Dean nodded. "I love you too, Mama. I'm glad I'm home now." A few tears fell and a weight felt as if it was lifted. Dax and his *mom still loved him, they hadn't rejected him or kicked him out. They were giving him a home, a new start. A better one. And suddenly he felt hopeful again, the ground a little less shaky.*

Dax and Mama Beth had taken him in that day, and he'd become part of the family. He'd lived with them until he'd gone to college to get his teaching degree while Dax had gone into basic training. Dean had gotten a job as an English teacher at the middle school just last year right before Dax had gone on his second deployment. They'd had a hell of a celebration, for Dean's dream job and Dax popping the question to Jessie. Everything had been good, until now. He should go to Beth's, he wanted to be with his mama. She had to be devastated and Dax would have kicked his ass for what he had done—he had lost it and she had to be wondering what had happened and why the call had ended. They'd definitely need each other to get through this.

Except he didn't even want to move. He just stared up at the sky. "Damn you, Dax, I *told* you to be careful! How the *hell* am I supposed to do this without you?"

It was a few more minutes but he forced himself to move. Mama needed him. He'd run some more, right to her house. Hopefully he'd get himself under control so he could be strong and take care of her. That's what Dax would want and he had made him a promise.

Chapter Two

"Could you get that box, baby?" Mama asked him. "I think that's the last one."

"Sure, Mama." Dean looked around the now empty apartment. Jessie had moved back in with her parents, since the apartment was on post and she couldn't stay there any longer. Dean had volunteered to help pack things up alone, not wanting Beth or Jessie to have to, but his mom was stubborn so they'd tackled the daunting task together with both tears and laughter. He picked up the box. Inside was a Go Army T-shirt, Dax's dog tags, and a picture of him with his buddies in Afghanistan.

"I still write Jerry and Damian," she told him.

"You do?"

"Mm, bless their hearts. They're good boys." She dusted off her hands. "Dax told me they didn't have family, so what else could I do but keep writing them? They're going through hell. They need to know they've got people who care."

Dean kissed her cheek. He was proud of her and knew how lucky he was that she'd taken him under her wing. That's who Beth was—a mother and a nurturer through and through. "Maybe I should do that too then."

Mama smiled. "You should. I know you miss him as much as I do. It helps a little, and I think it's a good way to honor his memory. He'd want us to support his buddies and remember what he gave his life for. That's what I keep telling myself anyway."

"You're right, Mama. I think it'd make Dax happy to know you're keeping in touch with them."

Dean tucked the box under his arm and walked out with her. Besides his fellow teachers he was seriously lacking in the friend department. Without Dax, he was alone but not interested in hanging out and making friends at the local bar. He was too shy for that—hell, that's why he was still single. Without Dax dragging him places, he preferred to stay in the world of literature and escape the current reality. But he could do this for Dax, it'd be a way to do something for him. Writing letters was right up his alley. Maybe he could help someone out, make a friend and start the healing process. And maybe, just maybe make the ache in his chest hurt a little less. Though he wasn't counting on that last one.

* * * *

Hey Ryder,

So, uh, I've never really done this. I mean I had a pen pal when I was, like, eight, and I waited for the mailman every day to see what Skylar would say about kangaroos in Australia. Everything is so techy now, you know, email, texts, and written letters are rare. I guess that was part of the appeal, this just feels more important taking the time to write by hand. And you deserve that.

The reason I decided to become a pen pal is I recently lost my brother and, well, I thought in his memory I'd do more to give back and find ways to support guys like him going through hell over there and fighting for our country. I want to say thanks, and I honestly do admire you. I don't think I could do it. I'm a creature of comfort and complain ridiculously when it's hot.

Anyway, I keep going on about me. Thanks for everything you're doing. I hope you're staying safe. I'm sure you got a lot going on so if I don't hear from you it's okay. I just wanted to let you know I'm thinking of you and wishing you a safe journey home.

Take care,
Dean

After sealing the letter into the envelope, Dean decided

he'd take his dog for a walk since he had to put it in the mailbox. The weather was a little chilly as fall was just beginning, but he loved this time of year. He grabbed a jacket and the leash hanging by the door. He tucked the letter in his pocket then whistled.

"Sassy! C'mere, girl!"

Sassy, his three-year-old Jack Russell terrier, dashed down the hall and skidded to a stop beside him. A fellow teacher, Michael, volunteered at the local shelter and last year he'd told Dean about Sassy, abandoned and left on post. One visit and he'd been in love with the little diva and taken her home. She was a firecracker and fiercely protective of him now. When she saw what he was holding, she stood up on her hind legs and whined. With a chuckle, he knelt and attached the hook to her collar, getting excited kisses and paws.

"All right, sit." It was nearly impossible to do with her so bouncy. She gave him her big brown puppy eyes but sat, tail wagging like mad. He made sure the leash was secure, rubbed her ears then stood.

He opened the door and stepped onto the porch. He stuck the letter in the mailbox and went for their walk. They took their time, Sassy had unlimited energy and could walk all day. He strolled through the park, stopped for a coffee and got her a bowl of water before heading home.

Jessie was on the front porch with Bones, Dax's German Shepherd. The feeling of refreshment from the brisk weather was replaced by worry. "Is everything, okay?"

"Sort of." Jessie brushed her curly red hair back behind her ears. "I've got a huge favor to ask."

"Name it," Dean said with a smile. "Actually, let's get the monsters inside first."

Jessie followed him in through the front entry. He went down the hall into the kitchen–dining room and pulled open the sliding door. Once Bones and Sassy were free from their leashes they chased each other out. He shut it quickly behind them. "Now we can talk. You want some tea? Coffee?"

"Coffee, please." Jessie took a seat on the bar stool, watching as he rummaged around and started making coffee. "So, um... You know how I took the graveyard shift at the hospital?"

"Yep, better pay, right?" Dean knew she hoped to get her own place as soon as possible. He had offered to let her stay with him as he had a spare room but she'd wanted to be with her mom.

"Yeah, well, Bones isn't handling things very well. My dad won't let Bones sleep in their room while I'm at work and I think he's lonely, so he, uh, howls, like, all night. I know it's a lot to ask but could you take him for a while?"

"Sure, he gets along with Sassy. I don't see it being a problem." Dean glanced out at the yard. "Poor guy. He knows something's wrong."

"He does. He seems so sad." Jessie sighed, swiping at her jade green eyes. "Whenever I start crying he lays his head in my lap and lets me hug him. Damn, I don't want to let him go. I wish I didn't have to..."

"Hey." Dean went around the counter and put his arm around her. "He's not going anywhere. He'll be right here and you know you're welcome any time."

She turned and hugged him, her face buried in his neck. He felt a few tears fall onto his collar. "I miss him, too."

She sniffled and pulled back. "I'm sorry, Dean. I just got Dax's stuff today and he left me a letter in his gear bag..." She dug into her jean pocket. "He left one for you, too."

Dean took the folded letter with a trembling hand. Dax's goodbye, well, he was going to need something stronger than coffee to read it. He stopped the coffee maker, then grabbed two beers from the fridge. Jessie gave him a watery smile and they toasted the longnecks as he sat beside her.

"To Dax," they said in unison.

"You don't have to read it while I'm here if you don't want to."

Dean shook his head. "I don't want to read it alone."

She peeled the label on the bottle. "He was real sweet and it was just what I needed, but damn, I was counting on forever with him. Now I'll never know." She stared down at the engagement ring that she had yet to take off.

"I'm so sorry, Jessie." Dean stubbornly fought back tears as he unfolded the letter and started reading.

Dean,

If you're reading this I just broke my promise to you and I'm not coming home. I'm sorry, little bro, I never wanted to break a promise to you or let you down.

Take care of Mama. I know she'll be all right 'cause she has you. And Jessie too, tell her that I loved her with all I had and I hope she never forgets me because she was the love of my life. But I don't want her mourning me forever. She's too beautiful to be alone and sad.

Don't you dare go mourning me forever either. I'll find some way back, like, as a ghost or something. So if you feel a boot to your ass it's me.

You get out and do the stuff I never got to. Go traveling some more. Have a beer for me. And cheer on our team. Just have fun, k? Be spontaneous and do something crazy without me. That's all I want, for you to be happy. And don't be afraid, you've always been the stronger one, you just didn't know it. You can get through this, I know it.

You were the best brother I could ever ask for. I'll be with you always... Dax

It was Jessie's turn to hug him as he cried. The letter let loose the tumult of emotions he'd kept bottled up, and he felt drained yet better once the tears had stopped flowing. He took a swig of beer and rubbed at his eyes. He wished he'd had a chance to say that Dax had saved him all those years ago, and he didn't know where he'd be if he hadn't. Even though Dax knew that, he still would have given anything just to say goodbye and to tell Dax he'd never let him down. He skimmed over the letter again, intending to do as Dax asked, then smiled at Jessie. "We may have not gotten enough time with him, but we were lucky to have the time that we did."

"Best year of my life," Jessie agreed.

"Thanks for bringing me the letter." Dean folded it reverently then got up and placed it next to a picture of him and Dax on a side table. "You know, I wrote to a pen pal today, too."

"Like Beth does?"

"Yep." Dean turned back to her. "I don't know if he'll even write me back, but I guess that was spontaneous, huh?"

"Yeah, it is."

"I definitely don't want a ghost boot kicking my butt so I'll have to cheer on the Royals later, too," he joked, making Jessie laugh.

Chapter Three

Camp Nathan Smith, Afghanistan

"Sergeant Brooks, you've got a letter." James held out an envelope to Ryder. He took it with a thanks and the private continued calling out names.

For a moment, Ryder wondered who could be writing to him, then he remembered the pen pal program. He'd set an example for his men, knowing that some of them were lonely just like he was. He hoped it made them feel good, it was sure nice to know someone had taken the time to write to him. Though, truth be told, he didn't think it'd help. He was gay—he wasn't interested in talking to women. And if it was a guy, what could they possibly talk about? What were the chances of him finding someone he had even one thing in common with? And he certainly didn't need any more homophobic asses or closet cases to deal with—he had enough of those already.

With a sigh, he went back to his tent and ducked inside. He sank onto the cot and stared at the letter. Liking ripping off a Band-Aid he decided to just get it over with. Maybe he'd get lucky—he sure could use a friend. Someone to talk to without having to worry about what he said. But again he was doubtful.

Still, he unfolded the single sheet of paper. The writing stopped his thoughts. The penmanship was elegant—long, flowing script filled the page. He noticed the name, 'Dean', and realized it was a guy. He had to be a writer or poet with that kind of handwriting.

He read the letter, feeling Dean's hurt and loss for his

brother as if he knew him. Maybe he had. Maybe he hadn't, but he still had been a brother in battle and Ryder sent up a brief prayer for him.

He read it again, a smile quirking his lips and he almost laughed about the kangaroo.

So he'd been wrong. He was glad now he had signed up, because Dean had reminded him of home. The reasons he was fighting. The hope he felt. His spirits lifted and he realized he had needed this. He needed a friend, someone not connected to everything around him who he could just talk to. He grabbed his gear bag, searching for the notepad and pen, then he scribbled down a reply. His handwriting was nowhere near as beautiful as Dean's but it was eligible at least.

Hey Dean,

Thanks for the letter. First time my name got called during mail call and, boy, I'll tell you, it made me feel pretty damn good. I guess I've been trying to ignore the loneliness like I did on the last tour, but it's nice to know someone is thinking about me. Makes me glad I caved and put my name on the pen pal list.

So, I'm sorry to hear about your brother. I've lost a few myself here. Never gets any easier. Though it makes me fight harder. I, uh, never really had any family. Foster kid. I joined the Army as soon as I was able and it became my family, and these guys are my brothers. So I give it all I got and hope I make them proud. You don't have to thank me for doing this, I'm glad to. Makes me feel like I got a purpose and I'm doing something important.

I'd like to hear more about you. Where do you work? What do you like to do? Any news from back home? I miss good coffee and watching NASCAR. I don't much like the heat here either, but compared to everything else going on it's easy to ignore. I'm sure I'm not as interesting as Skylar, only sand and flies here. No kangaroos, but I hope you'll write me again anyway. It's nice having someone to talk to. Like I said it gets lonely here. I'm keeping busy, though, I've got to lead the guys on patrol in a few minutes so I have to wrap this up.

All the best,
Ryder

He'd have to get an envelope later. For now he folded up both letters, tucked them in his shirt pocket, grabbed his cap then got back to work.

Chapter Four

Hey Ryder,

Well, I can't say how happy you made me to know I cheered you up a little. Totally made me smile. I'm going to keep on writing you to chase away that loneliness and make sure your name gets called each time the mail comes. Sound good?

Thanks, I miss Dax like crazy. He was a good friend and an even better brother. I, uh, lost my family when I was sixteen. Dax and his family took me in and gave me a place to belong. He never judged and was always there for me. I miss him, I miss going out for a beer every Friday night and playing pool. Man, just writing this is making me hurt. Dax always had my back and I'm not sure I'll ever get over this feeling like there's a hole in my heart. Damn, you don't need to hear me being depressing and sad. Sorry about that.

I'm sure you're making everyone proud. I think the attitude you have is great. Definitely important to have a purpose and feel like you're making a difference. I'm a teacher at a junior high so I know that feeling. Encouraging and helping kids is what I love to do. I'm kinda boring otherwise. I like to read a lot, I travel occasionally because I'm a history buff, and my Saturday nights are spent playing Scrabble with my friends. Just your average guy.

NASCAR, huh? I don't usually watch it but for you I'll watch the race this week and let you know how it goes. I'm sending you a care package with a bunch of coffee blends, I wasn't sure which one you preferred. Let me know and I'll send more. Oh I don't know, I'd say you have Skylar beat. He wrote me twice, both times he asked me silly questions and refused to ship me my own kangaroo even after I mailed him my allowance. Which he kept by the way. The joys of being a kid.

I sent you some fly strips too. And a book. I figured it'd help pass the time? If you think it's boring just toss it and let the sand bury it.

I hope you're staying safe. Take care, I'll write again soon.
Dean

* * * *

Hey Dean,
Sorry for taking so long to write back. I hope you didn't worry too much, I'm all right. I can't say much but it's been a rough week. I know we've only written a few letters but just writing this now is making me feel better knowing I have you to talk to.

It's okay if you wanna talk about Dax. I don't mean to pry, but I'm sorry you lost your family. That's great Dax's took you in. I'd give all I have to have a real family, maybe one day I will start my own. I already know what not to do. Anyway, I imagine if I had time to think about it I'd be feeling the loss of my buddies too. But when I'm doing a mission that grief and hurt gets stuffed in my pack and I move on to accomplish the mission. That's all I can do right now. Gotta have a clear head. Anyways, I've been known to play a mean game of pool, but I'm too far away for that right now.

Yeah exactly, this is what I'm meant to do. Not sure I'd even be good at anything else. I like architecture, think about that every now and then. I even have a sketchpad. But this is my job and I love it. And you don't sound boring to me at all. Teaching kids is a special gift. And quiet Saturday nights, man, I do miss those. It's so loud here and I can never completely relax or unwind. Ah, well. Have a beer for me, would ya?

So, I hope I'm not crossing a line here but, uh, is there anyone special in your life? You don't have to answer if you don't want to. I'm just curious to know more about you. And I'm single, but I'm sure you guessed that already what with me going on about being lonely.

Who won the race? If you watched, and if you didn't that's okay. And wow, those coffees! I'm not sure which one to pick as I liked them all. Maybe another batch of assorted would be good. I appreciate it – coffee keeps me awake on patrol at night. And those fly strips are just what we need.

I haven't laughed in a while but that sure felt good. I'm sorry he didn't send you a kangaroo. The least he could've done was send a stuffed one. Though I guess that would've been just as disappointing with it not being the real thing, huh?

We sure do have a lot in common. I like historical books – not quite a buff about events and people but I could talk your ear off about landmarks and ancient architecture. Thanks, it helped pass some time.

I hope you're doing all right. Take care.
Ryder

Chapter Five

Dean had liked talking to Ryder these past few weeks, letters going back and forth. Ryder seemed to be a great guy, and someone Dean enjoyed getting to know. A friend. Writing to Ryder had made him smile when nothing else could. Now he feared losing that as he wasn't going to lie about his sexuality. Ever since he had gone through the hell of losing his family he had refused to be anything other than who he was. And he didn't hide it. The school knew he was gay, some of the students did as well. He'd even helped a few kids start an anti-bullying group and mentored in hopes of being there for them in case their families turned their backs on them like his had done.

But how would Ryder react? Would he write to him again? Or would he lose a friend? With a sigh he crumpled up a sheet of paper and started the letter over. There was only one way to find out.

Hey Ryder,

It was good to hear from you. I was worried, been watching the news and hoping you were safe. I'm glad you are. Sure we have only written a few times but I think of you as a friend already and hope you feel the same.

I get that. You gotta stay focused on the mission so you can complete it and come home. When is your tour over? Maybe we could have a beer and shoot some pool. And you can totally tell me no if you were kidding about that.

Architecture, huh? Well, I found some books for you and I'm

*actually taking a trip down to Savannah next month and visiting
a cousin. So, I'll take some pics there and send you some of the old
houses, churches, and other landmarks. Have you ever traveled
to Europe? I love exploring ruins and castles, went backpacking
once before I started teaching. That was an amazing trip.*

*I will have a beer for you and toast in your honor. All that noise
would probably drive me crazy. I hope you're getting enough rest.*

*You're not crossing a line. I'm single too. And, uh, gay. I guess
since I told you that I can tell you I got kicked out of my parents'
home for being gay. Dax knew and pulled me up from what felt
like rock bottom at the time. He was the reason I didn't go back in
the closet or wind up on the streets or worse…*

*I just want you to know I didn't sign up for this to hook up
with a soldier. Although one can dream. Kidding! I did it for the
friendship, honestly. I guess I'll, uh, see what your response is
before I go any further with this topic.*

*You're welcome, I'm glad I didn't bore you with the book. More
coffee, some books, and fly strips are headed your way. Let me
know if you need anything else, 'kay?*

Take care and stay safe,
Dean

* * * *

Camp Nathan Smith, Afghanistan

Ryder felt a grin splitting his face as he read the letter.
Dean was gay. He could talk to him and he'd understand.
He wouldn't lose their friendship over it. And maybe,
well… Maybe there could even be more later on. He knew
it was a little crazy to even think it but just writing to Dean
he felt a connection. Something special. Dean was special.
Ryder could see that in the letters, how kind and caring
Dean was. The big heart he had. He wanted to meet him,
thank him for all he'd done these past few weeks.

Hey Dean,
Let me start by saying this: I'm gay too. I believe you and I

know you're sincere because I did this for the friendship as well. You don't know how hard it is to keep who I am hidden away sometimes. Sure, DADT is dead, but prejudices aren't. It's still tough to be a gay man in the military. A few of my friends know but my CO is a homophobic ass so I stay quiet and keep my head down. Besides, my life is private and separate from what goes on here. Just like our letters — they're mine and I keep them close. Everyone else can think what they like, I don't care. I'm proud of who I am and they won't change me.

Damn, I'll never understand parents who do stuff like that. You can't change who you are and they should have loved you. It's their loss in my opinion. I'm sure your family now sees what they didn't and are proud. I think you're amazing, kindhearted, and no one has gotten me to laugh in months like you have…

I consider myself lucky that I got you as a pen pal, Dean. Honestly, I feel like we have a connection and it's nice to be able to talk to you about this and know you understand. We are friends. I wasn't kidding, I'd like to thank you in person when I get back home in seven months. If you want to meet that is.

That'd be great. Savannah is gorgeous this time of year. Old Fort Jackson and Forsyth Park are two of my favorite places. The history of that city, you can just feel it and it leaves you in awe. I could wander all day around the historic district and not get tired. See, I'm a secret geek. I've been to Germany on duty and Italy once but backpacking would be an amazing experience I bet.

Thanks. I am. I sleep like a log. I get so exhausted by the end of the day that as soon as I lay my head down I'm out cold.

I will let you know if I need anything. Right now that's perfect.
Take care,
Ryder

Ryder nearly jumped out of his skin when Bentley tapped him on his shoulder. Instinctively his hand went to a knife he had hidden in his boot. He relaxed as his friend held up his hands and took a step back.

"Whoa, man." Bentley chuckled. "I didn't realize you were spaced out there."

"I was just finishing up a letter."

"Dean?" Bentley asked with his usual nosiness.

"Yeah." Ryder stood and dropped his voice so only Ben could hear. "I thought the pen pal thing would be a waste of time. Turns out I was wrong. He's like me, Ben." *Like you too, not that you'll ever admit it.*

"Really? So you're going to meet him when we finally get outta here?"

"Maybe." Ryder shrugged. "I'm leaving it up to him."

With a frown, Bentley asked, "But you want to?"

Bentley didn't seem to like the idea but Ryder didn't care. Sure, he had Ben and a few other friends here but they were on a mission. Getting emotional and talking about their loneliness wouldn't help. And none of them would talk about that stuff anyway. But writing to Dean kept him from bottling it all up. "Yeah, I just can't explain it but I really want to. I need someone apart from all this. It helps."

"That's why I'm lucky I've got Rachel." Bentley folded his arms. "You know you should find a pretty girl. How do you expect to get any further up the chain if you're with some guy?"

"He's not just some guy," Ryder snapped. "We've been through this. I'm not hiding in a damn closet!" *Not like you. Not ever.*

"Your mistake, man." Bentley turned on his heel.

Ryder thought the biggest mistake he'd ever made was stupidly thinking he could change Bentley. He'd wasted years on the ass, thinking maybe Bentley would care enough to come out and be open with him. But no, that hadn't happened. Ryder had finally had enough and cut all ties outside the Army. Bentley was with a woman but that didn't mean he didn't secretly hook up with guys. Disgusted, Ryder shook his head, wondering why he'd ever thought he'd seen something in Bentley. But that was in the past. He was better off and had moved on a while ago.

He took out the letter. He was going to be more careful,

take his time and trust his instincts. Besides, Dean was everything Bentley wasn't. He was a good guy who was out and proud. He wouldn't hide Ryder away. He wouldn't keep things secret back home. He had a chance at something real.

Chapter Six

Savannah, Georgia

Dean was glad he'd decided to drive down to Georgia during his spring break. He and Dax had planned road trips but never got around to them. The drive was a bit lonely but worth it. When he got to Savannah it was late so he crashed at his cousin's. The next day, he took his camera, some books, and went exploring all over the city. In the morning, he walked all around the Historic District, snapping photos as much for himself as for Ryder. He had a sandwich in Forysth Park, went to an art museum, met his cousin Peter and his wife, Jenna, for dinner and before calling it a night he went out for drinks at a little hole in the wall bar.

He'd just ordered a Scotch when a handsome blond sat on the stool next to him. Dark green eyes met his as a hand was held out. "Jake. Is this seat taken?"

"Dean. No I'm here on my own."

Interest flared in the man's eyes and Dean was both surprised and intrigued. It'd been a long time since he'd fooled around or hooked up. "So am I. Having a good night?"

"Great actually, I'm visiting family and did all sorts of touristy stuff today."

"Nice. Just got off work myself. Paralegal." Jake smiled and sipped his beer. "Just wanted to unwind, y'know?"

Dean did. Except he couldn't follow through. Ryder. He thought of him, and his interest in Jake was lost. They'd been writing letters for over a month now. They planned to meet as soon as Ryder got home and Dean wanted that. More than he could say. Ryder had eased the pain and loneliness. And their connection — well, he wanted to see if that spark would come alive when they finally met face to face. He couldn't jeopardize any of that with a meaningless fling. They hadn't talked about it, but there was the promise of a relationship there. He just had to be patient.

"I do but I can't. Sorry."

"You seeing someone?"

Dean didn't know how to answer that but he said, "Kind of. It's complicated."

Jake raised an eyebrow at him. "How so, if you don't mind my asking?"

"He's in the military. Deployed right now."

"Ah hell, I'd be a real jerk then if I kept hitting on you while your guy is over there. Sorry."

"It's okay." Dean smiled. "Long story but we started writing letters and just clicked, y'know? I want there to be something when he gets home but..."

Jake turned to him in obvious shock. "Wow, so you haven't even met?"

Dean's face heated up. "No, but I think I already know him better than most guys I've dated."

With a whistle, Jake said, "He must be something special for you to want to wait."

"He is. I'm sorry for rambling on, I'm sure you're a good guy too but—"

"I'm not him." Jake clapped his shoulder. "No hard feelings. Tell him I appreciate everything he does for our country, all right?" He glanced over his shoulder. "Blue eyes over there is giving me a look, I'm gonna go say hi. Enjoy your vacation."

"Thanks, I will." Dean flashed him a smile. "Have fun."

"Oh I will," Jake said with a chuckle as he got up from his bar stool.

Dean paid for his drink, left the bar and took a taxi to Peter's. He snuck in quietly as they'd already gone to bed and went to his room to change and get ready to crash himself.

After a quick shower, he slipped on a pair of sweats and a T-shirt. His iPhone started ringing from the dresser and when he grabbed it he was surprised to see an international number. Daring to hope it was Ryder, he answered.

"Hello?"

A voice as sweet as honey replied, "Dean?"

Dean clutched the phone as he sank down on the bed. "Ryder?"

"Yeah, it's me. Look I only got a few minutes but I just wanted to call and hear your voice."

"It's good to finally hear yours." Dean grinned and settled back against the headboard.

"Yours too. How's your day been? Enjoying Savannah?"

"Loving it. I took so many pictures. It's been an amazing day, I can't wait to do more tomorrow."

Ryder chuckled. "I'm glad. Did you have a beer for me?"

"Scotch." Dean paused, wondering how he could broach the subject. "Ryder, um, can I ask you something?"

"Anything."

"Are we… Are we kind of together?" Dean said in a rush, feeling his throat tighten. "It feels like we are, even though we're apart."

"Well, I can't ask you to wait five months for me. But yeah, I'd like us to see where things could go when I get home if you still want to then."

Dean let out a breath he hadn't realized he'd been holding. "I'm waiting, you don't have to ask."

"Then we are together," Ryder said and Dean could hear the happiness in his voice.

"Good, 'cause I totally blew off some guy earlier at the bar and told him I was seeing a guy who was deployed."

Ryder laughed. "Seriously?" His voice dropped into a lower register that sent a shiver down Dean's spine. "Dean, I'm real glad you did."

"Yeah? Me too, I wouldn't have wanted to miss your call.

And it didn't feel right." He paused as he realized Ryder had gone quiet. "Ry?"

"Oh I like you calling me that," Ryder said softly. "Sorry, I'm kinda blown away here that you turned down a guy when you haven't even seen a picture of me."

"Does this mean I get to now? I was going to send you some of me here. Wait, should I? I know you said your CO was a dick."

"Yeah, screw him. I want a photo. I'll hide it. And I'll get you one, too."

Dean broke into a smile as he crawled under the covers. "Great, I wish we could talk longer. Time's almost up, huh?"

"You know the drill, yeah, just a minute or so."

"It was easy, you know. I don't care that we haven't met. We've connected, talked for weeks. I know you and that it'll be worth waiting for you to get home," Dean confessed, unable to stop himself. "You'd best be careful and get back to me."

"I will, I promise." Ryder paused. "I'll call you again when I can."

"Do you need anything?"

"Just the usual. I guess you couldn't mail yourself over here," Ryder teased.

"For a quickie?" Dean laughed. "Tempting. I don't suppose you can talk dirty to me?"

"Probably be frowned upon," Ryder said, and Dean could hear the grin in his voice. "Shoot, I gotta go. Take care, Dean."

"You too, Ry."

The call disconnected and Dean felt the loss. He could've talked to Ryder for hours, just listening to his voice and enjoying their conversation. He set his alarm and was going to put the phone on the nightstand when it pinged an email. He opened it and a grin split his face as he saw a picture of his soldier. Ryder was standing with some of his men, dressed in his fatigues. He was as tall and strong as Dean imagined. And his eyes were a gorgeous shade of green. Dean ran his fingers over the picture. There was an easy smile on Ryder's face and Dean wished there weren't oceans separating them.

Dream of me tonight. Ryder xx

With a quick reply, Dean sent a picture of himself.

I'll see you there. Dean xx

* * * *

Dean heard the door creak open and blearily turned his head, stunned to see Ryder there. His solider was quickly taking off his uniform, seeming to be in a haste to get to him. Dean sat up, cupping Ryder's face in his hands when he reached him. After he pulled Ryder on top of him, their lips met in a fiery kiss that left him aching for more. He felt the hard planes and muscles of Ryder's strong body pressing him into the mattress and loved it. He thrust up as their cocks bumped together. Groaning into Ryder's mouth, Dean grabbed Ryder's ass, clutching it, desperate for whatever Ryder would give him.

"Please," he whimpered.

With a grin, Ryder reached down, taking Dean in his calloused hand. "We got all night, baby. Nice and slow."

Dean liked that idea and nodded, throwing his head back as Ryder stroked him from base to tip, spreading pre-cum that leaked from the tip. Ryder drove him crazy with the slow, teasing touches. Fire pooled in his gut and his body was taut, ready for release.

"Come for me, Dean." Ryder kissed him softly.

With a gasp, Dean woke with a start. He groaned as he realized it had been just a dream. A damn good one, but a dream nonetheless. His cock tented his sleep pants, hard and needing attention. He didn't want a cold shower, so he quietly took himself in hand, pushing down his pants, and recalled his fantasy. It didn't take much. He bit back a cry as cum spilled in his hand as he pictured Ryder and that sexy smile of his. He lay there for a minute, basking in the glow of his climax. Then he got up to clean himself up. Damn. It was going to be a long five months.

Chapter Seven

Alert and tense, Ryder strode through the bazaar, amazed at how people went about their lives as if they weren't in a war zone. Kids played in the streets, men and women perused stalls and bought wares all around him. Bentley and Joel were a ways ahead as he stopped at a stall, watching an old man whittle away. Dozens of carved wooden animals were laid out on a blanket. He knelt and picked up a tiger, detailed so beautifully Ryder almost purchased it until he thought of Dean and another idea sprang to mind.

Taking his notepad and a pen from his pocket, he then drew a kangaroo, and approached the man who carried on with his work, ignoring the gun by Ryder's side. Ryder passed him the paper and pointed to the carvings. The man took it, a questioning look on his face for a moment then he nodded in understanding. He put the monkey he was carving down, grabbed a piece of wood and put the paper over it.

"Yes," Ryder said with a nod of his own. "How much?" He took off his sports watch and again got a nod. Followed by the man picking up a cup with tepid coffee and pointing to it. He'd have to get a package back on base. "Deal." He held out his hand and the elderly guy shook it. He then pointed to the sun and held up two fingers so Ryder figured he'd return in two hours for the kangaroo. With a grin, he gave the man the watch as a deposit and left him to whittle, continuing on down the street through the bazaar. Now he thought about whether he'd send it to Dean or better yet save it and give it to him in person in two months.

* * * *

Wandering slowly through the cemetery, Dean made his way to Dax's gravestone. He crouched down, brushing away the leaves and placing a beer next to it.

"Happy Birthday, Dax." Dean sat on his heels, tracing his fingers over the cold stone. He popped the cap on the beer, took a swig then poured some into the ground. "I miss you so much."

Silence. Just silence. Dax had always been talkative, loud, he didn't like it when it was quiet. Sometimes it had bothered Dean as he liked the peace and to just take it all in. He'd give anything now to hear Dax's nonstop chatter.

"I kind of feel weird talking to you like this," he admitted hoarsely. "You know I'm not religious, but I hope you're in a good place. I like to think you're watching over me." He blinked away the moisture in his eyes. "I think you are. It was because of you that I met Ryder…"

A few tears fell despite his effort to hold them in. "I was so angry at first with you, Dax. I begged you to leave the Army, to not go back on that second tour. I knew why you had to go but I was so scared and look what happened! You broke your promise, you left me. You left us all and we've had to pick up the pieces."

He paused and picked at the label on the beer. "I'm not angry now. Just sad… You gave me a family and love when I had no one, Dax. And I'll never forget that or all our good times together. I'm taking care of Mom and watching out for Jessie. But I wish you were here. There's so much you didn't get to do. It's unfair. But I'm gonna do my best to make you proud and do the things you can't now.

"I'm taking the chances you wanted me to. I think you'd like Ryder. I'm real excited to meet him. We've got this connection. And his voice when I hear it… I get it now when you said you just knew Jessie was special. That she was the one. I haven't met Ryder but I know he's special. I know too I couldn't have gotten through losing you without him."

Dean sighed. "He's a soldier, y'know. I'm terrified now that there's only a month left until he can come home. What if something happens?" He swallowed hard around the lump in his throat. "I'm not sure I could handle that... Could you watch over him too? Bring him home to me." He shook his head. "I must be crazy, but maybe I just want to believe you're still around..."

Dean started as a few drops of rain fell on him. "Mom loves that song about there being holes in the floor of heaven, and a person's tears are falling because they wish they could be here now." He gazed at the sky. "Wherever you are, I hope you're at peace, Dax. Don't worry about us. We'll be all right until we see you again."

As he pulled his coat collar up, Dean ran toward his car as the rain started to pour. He hadn't brought an umbrella so he dashed to his Saturn and climbed inside.

Chapter Eight

Dean watched his students, broken into groups, working on their essays for their book reports. His phone buzzed in his desk drawer. No one ever called during school hours. It seemed as if his heart stopped as he pulled the phone out and saw the number Ryder usually called from. He stood abruptly.

"Everyone, I've got an emergency call. I'll be outside the door. If I hear commotion or see anyone out of their seats, you'll get an automatic detention, no question." He walked to the door. "Keep working, I won't be long." *I hope.*

He accepted the call as he stepped out. Shaky and nauseated he managed a "Hello?"

"Dean." Ryder's voice sounded off but the world still slotted back into place hearing it.

"Ry, thank God. Are you all right? What's happened?"

"Oh damn, you're teaching, aren't you? I'm sorry."

"No, it's okay as long as you are," Dean said, trying to take calming breaths.

"It's been the worst day... I just needed to hear you," Ryder admitted softly. "I can call you back. I don't want you getting in trouble."

"No, I can take a few minutes." Dean trusted his students — they were the advanced lit course and well behaved. And they knew he hadn't been kidding as he'd never threatened detention before.

"You sure?"

"Positive. Want to talk about it?"

"Just a rough day. Bentley was giving me crap as we patrolled. Turns out I was right about something. It ended up all right but…"

Dean clutched the phone tighter. He leaned against the wall. "Not hurt, are you?"

"Not even a scratch," Ryder assured. "Yesterday, though, we lost a few guys in another patrol. Everyone's on edge and today just made it worse. I just want to take five."

Realizing that Ryder needed his support and a little comfort, Dean pulled himself together. "Can you close your eyes?"

"I might look a little silly but sure."

"Okay, so close 'em. And I want you to tune it all out. Just focus on my voice."

"'Kay. I wish you were here, Dean."

Dean had been told a time or two that he had a nice singing voice and suddenly lyrics from one of Beth's favorite songs popped into his head. He hummed softly, and sang the chorus to Lonestar's *I'm Already There*. He purposely changed 'love' to 'feel', but he wanted to say that word when he could touch, kiss, and hold his soldier. He was in love with him, though, he'd known it for a while. It didn't matter that they hadn't met.

Ryder was still silent and Dean waited anxiously. Then he said, "I like that song. Damn, time's almost up."

"Yeah, I gotta get back inside," Dean agreed. "Just remember that, okay? If it gets too rough on you again."

"I will, baby," Ryder's voice dropped to a whisper. "Thanks for knowing what I needed."

"Anytime." Dean broke into a smile, happiness bubbling up. Ryder had never called him anything other than his name before. *Baby. I didn't think I'd like being called that, but the way Ryder said it. Damn.* Clearly the song had meant something to him too. "Call me later?"

"I'll try my best. If not, tomorrow for sure."

"Okay, take care, babe."

Now Dean could hear a grin in Ryder's voice. Mission accomplished. "I will. Bye."

The call disconnected and, still floating on a cloud, Dean

headed back into class.

* * * *

Ryder stared at the phone for a long minute. He was glad he was alone in the tent and no one else was making calls, he needed some time to put the mask back in place and carry on.

He'd had the day from hell. Quick thinking had saved Bentley's ass and prevented disaster. His nerves had been shot, and he'd nearly lost his temper. Then he'd called Dean. Just hearing him calmed him down. He felt bad for worrying him. But Dean really had given him something special just now. A peace had washed over him when Dean started singing, then he had listened to the words, and the emotion in Dean's voice. How had a shy English teacher oceans away stolen his heart?

Maybe it was because no one, ever in his life, had been there solely for *him*. No expectations, no demands, no pressure. Dean didn't ask for anything, he just gave freely. His time. His affection. His support. For the first time, he felt *wanted* and in turn he *needed* Dean. How the heck had he gotten so lucky?

Closing his eyes, he again pictured Dean. Wrapping him up in his arms and never letting go. Two months. Two months and he could do that. All he had to do was get through this and go home.

Chapter Nine

It was another day closer to going home. Thirty-two days and a wake-up and he'd be gone. Home. To Dean. Ryder knew better than to push his luck by counting down days but he had been.

A routine patrol. Like any other day. They'd been following a lead that hadn't panned out, no insurgents in the village. They'd found an abandoned house on the outskirts and he'd had them search the area. There was a shed in the back, as dilapidated as the house. Ryder caught a glint of metal in the sunlight from a hole in the wood.

"Show yourselves or I shoot!" he warned.

Two men burst out, assault rifles at the ready. He jumped in front of his guys, firing his gun and wounding one fatally. The other he hit in the arm and the gun fell. The man reached for the weapon, and Ryder fired the kill shot before anyone else could.

He glanced around the rocky terrain. They were too damned exposed out here. "Let's go, guys. Before any other fuckers show up."

Allen grabbed the guns the men had had, then they started trekking back toward the village.

They had just reached the road. Ryder saw Private Martinez freeze mid-step, sweat immediately breaking out on his temples. Ryder cursed as he spotted the mine mostly hidden beneath the packed dirt. Martinez's left foot was planted in the center of it.

"Sarge, I got a problem." Martinez gulped. "I really did it this time."

"Nobody move!" Ryder ordered, carefully approaching

Joel. "It's all right, Private. I'll get you outta this."

Bentley joined Ryder. If he couldn't disarm this thing, nobody could. Bentley pulled out his pocket knife, and studied the mine. Ryder knew they were screwed when Bentley glanced up at him. "Damn it, it'll go off if I mess with it. Hell, we probably shouldn't even be breathing on it."

Ryder glared at Bentley. Joel was barely holding it together. They could all see that and the private certainly didn't need to hear that. "Mathers, shut up. Clear the men out now."

Bentley clearly wanted to argue. Of course he did. "But—"

"Orders, Specialist Mathers. Now!" Ryder stood and gently put a hand on Joel's shoulder. "We're going to get these guys out then you and me are going to have a nice sprint, Joel."

Joel chewed on his lip. "Amelia was just born, Sarge. I haven't even held her yet."

That tore Ryder up inside. He'd never had a father. He couldn't let a little girl have a lonely childhood like he did. He didn't know how he was getting Joel out of this mess but he would. He only hoped he'd get to see Dean when it was all said and done. "I know but you will. I promise. Just pull yourself up by those bootstraps."

Joel managed a grin, though it was tinged with fear. "Yes, sir."

Bentley gestured to Reynolds and Allen and the three jogged away. Ryder knew Ben would make the call for help and prayed that he and Joel would somehow survive this. "You ready, Private? On my count I want you to run like hell. Run to Amelia, you got me?"

"Yes, sir." Joel's voice quivered slightly but he seemed determined now.

Ryder squeezed his shoulder. On the count of three they ran, the mine detonating as Joel dove down a hill toward safety. Ryder jumped onto him to shield him from the blast as shrapnel flew every which way. When he jumped, something hot and sharp sliced through his calf. He screamed in agony as he covered Joel. His ears rang, his vision was fuzzy. It hurt so badly. Worse than any pain he'd ever felt.

He waited a moment. Two. Then he rolled and tried to sit up. Blood gushed from a gaping wound, his leg severed almost off at the knee. He screamed again as Joel jumped up and Ryder hoped he was calling for help. He didn't know how Bentley was suddenly by his side but he was. He yanked off his belt and Ryder felt himself losing consciousness... There was so much blood.

He fell into Bentley's side. "Tell Dean," he whispered.

"Like hell, Ryder. You're not dying on me," Bentley shouted in his ear, holding onto his leg to stop the blood as he put pressure on the wound after tying the belt around his thigh. Ryder bit back another scream and tried again to focus on anything but his leg as Bentley did his best to help him.

He was dying... And he wouldn't be going home. To Dean. Dean. That thought played over and over in his mind as he heard a helicopter through the muffled noises. Was it coming to take him home? To Dean? He'd never even had a chance to hold him, kiss him. And wasn't that unfair?

Chapter Ten

Spring Lake, North Carolina

Back home—well, not home, as for nearly a month he'd been staring at the four walls of the hospital on base— Ryder folded the note and scrawled Dean's name across it. Dean was so close yet so far away. He'd thought it'd been fate that Dean lived near the base he was stationed at. Now, his heart felt like it was breaking. But it had to be done. He didn't want Dean seeing him like this. He didn't want him feeling obligated to stick around and be with a broken man.

Bentley stepped into his hospital room. He tossed Ryder a Snickers. "Got your favorite."

"Thanks." Ryder stared at the note. "Listen, I called you because I wanted to ask you a favor."

"Sure, what is it?"

Ryder had no one else so he was forced to ask Bentley since he couldn't leave the hospital. Dean deserved an explanation and he'd make sure he got one. He didn't want Dean thinking he'd stood him up. Of course, Dean wouldn't think that—he'd assume something was wrong and come searching for him. And he couldn't have that. Not when he was like this. "Dean is going to be waiting for me later today and I want you to give him this."

Bentley took the offered note. "Not going to meet him then?"

"Like this? Hell no."

Dropping into the chair beside him, Bentley then leaned forward. "I get it. Don't worry, I'll take care of it." He reached over for a second to cup Ryder's cheek. "You sure scared the hell out of me."

Ryder wanted to pull back but if he angered Bentley he might not do what he asked. So instead he said, "Thanks for what you did. You stopped me from bleeding to death."

"Anytime. I got your back even if you do hate me for what happened between us."

"I don't hate you. Not anymore." *I don't care about anything anymore.*

"I would. I'm sorry I couldn't be what you wanted." Bentley actually sounded sincere, which was surprising. "Dean's all right, from what you said. Maybe you should at least let him decide."

"No, I'm not putting this on him. Dean might have wanted a commitment from me but not like this. Just please deliver the message?"

"All right, well, no matter what happens, I'm here." Bentley leaned in farther and Ryder thought he might kiss him, which was the last thing he wanted. He wanted Dean's kisses but that was never going to happen. To add insult to injury, Bentley shuddered as he glanced down at Ryder's body and hurriedly stood. "What time?"

"Two. You should just make it."

"Okay, I'll figure out what to say. I'll come by afterward and let you know how it went."

"I don't want to know." Ryder curled his arms around himself, shrinking in as he saw the pity in Bentley's eyes. Even when he had wanted nothing to do with Bentley, he'd always had lust in his gaze. Now that was gone, replaced with a look that confirmed he was anything but attractive now. "Just go, please?"

* * * *

With a sigh, Dean glanced up at the clock on the far wall of the café. Ryder was nearly forty-five minutes late. Dean was starting to worry, his concern growing with every minute that passed. He hadn't heard from Ryder since his last letter over a month ago.

He glanced down at it in his hand.

Dean,

That was the sweetest thing you did having your students send my squad letters and cards. They sure cheered everyone up and brightened this drab area. You are gonna get a hug so big I'm gonna lift you off your feet when I see ya.

I can't believe I'll be home in less than five weeks and out of this hell. These past seven months have flown by. I couldn't have gotten through some days without you, Dean. I mean that. I just hope, when we meet, that spark comes alive. I can't wait to explore whatever this is between us. I've told you things I've never told anyone, and no one has cared for me like you.

Okay, I'll stop being a sap now and spoiling my rep as a badass soldier. I'm counting the days down, though. We'll meet at the café, all right? I'll be in my fatigues, and I'll leave post as soon as I can but if I'm a little late don't hold it against me.

If I don't get a chance to write you again or call, just know I'm thinking of you.

See you soon,

Ryder

Ryder had said a little late but Dean had a bad feeling. The kind he had just before that phone call from his mama. What if something awful had happened? How could he find out? Ryder didn't have any family, all he had was his squad. Maybe he could find them on base and ask. But could they tell him? Frustrated, Dean ran his hands down his thighs, trying to expel the nervous energy.

The door opened and Dean held his breath. He'd chosen this booth at the front to give him a clear view of people coming in. The blond guy was a soldier yet it wasn't Ryder. Fear twisted inside as the soldier headed toward him, a grim look etched across his face. Dean thought he might be sick. *Please God, not again.*

"Dean?" the man asked with a thick Texas drawl.

"Yeah, that's me. But who are you?" Dean held out his hand anyway, receiving a firm shake.

"I'm Bentley. Ben for short. It's nice to meet ya. Ryder talked about you quite a bit when we were on patrols together."

"He did?" Dean was surprised and touched. "Oh, you're Ben! He mentioned you before too. Sorry, I'm distracted."

"Mm, we're good friends," Bentley said with a sad smile. "It's why he asked me to do this." He pulled a letter from his breast pocket. "He's real sorry he can't be here."

With his hands shaking, Dean took the letter. He knew Ryder wanted to be here so what had prevented him from showing up? "Is he hurt?" he croaked. He just knew Ryder was—nothing else would've stopped him from being here. He knew Ryder cared for him, maybe even loved him. It's why he had waited anxiously every day until now for a letter or call. He'd thought maybe that Ryder had been on a mission or too busy readying for home, but deep down he'd known something was wrong when the constant communication had ended. His heart ached. Was he going to lose his chance at happiness before he even got to meet Ryder? Why was life so damn unfair?

Bentley slid into the booth on the opposite side. "I'm not supposed to say. He's in a real bad way and doesn't want you to see him like he is right now."

"I don't care!" Dean clutched the letter. "If he's hurt I want to see him. I need to know he's okay." *I'll go crazy otherwise.*

Shaking his head, Bentley replied, "He'd kick my ass from here to Iraq if I took you to the hospital."

Dean waited until Bentley met his gaze. "Tell me what happened."

"It's bad, like I said, Dean." Bentley stared down at his folded hands. "He's a real hero, though. Saved a guy in the explosion. But, uh." He cleared his throat. "He got his leg blown off..."

"Oh my God." Dean was grateful to be sitting down as the world tipped for a minute. "He's got to be hurting."

"Yeah, I mean he can push through the physical stuff but I think he's depressed," Bentley admitted. "He can't be a soldier now, he has months of rehab ahead of him, and he doesn't know what he's going to do."

"He needs help getting through all that. He can't do it alone."

"I tried telling him that. Didn't get very far. You don't got to worry, though, he's not alone. I've been looking out for him."

"That's good." Dean ran a hand through his hair. "So what? He thinks he'd be a burden to me now, right?"

Bentley simply nodded. "I believe his words were, 'Dean might have wanted a commitment from me but not like this'. I'm guessing the letter says that or something close to it."

Dean glanced at the letter, wondering if he should read it. Would it be an apology? He briefly skimmed over Ryder's writing.

Dean, I'm sorry. So sorry but I can't meet you today or any other day. Things have changed and it's better if you stay away. Just know I am grateful for what we shared even if it doesn't seem that way. Take care, I wish things had gone differently.

"Screw that." Dean stood. He took out his wallet and put some money on the table for his soda. "I'm not gonna let him go through this on his own. I'll find some way to get him to see that." *No way, I'm not giving up on him. Not a chance.*

Breaking into a grin, Bentley stood as well. "Well, I guess that means I'm taking you to the hospital?"

"Please." Dean tucked the letter in his wallet. "I know it's crazy, Bentley, because I've never even met Ryder, but he means something to me. I know him and even if it's as a friend I'm gonna be by his side for this no matter what."

"Then let's get you there." Bentley clapped him on the shoulder. "I care about Ryder. I can't get through to him but you can give it a shot."

Dean sure hoped so. He didn't want to think about what would happen if Ryder refused to let him visit.

Chapter Eleven

Ryder sat in the hospital bed listening to the clock ticking. Bentley should have delivered the letter by now, which meant Dean was likely upset and disappointed by it. As if Ryder could feel any worse. He hated what he had done. But what choice was there? His happiness had been right there, then it had slipped through his fingers again. There was something special between him and Dean. He had felt it even as they had been oceans apart. Each letter and call had made him smile and let him see another piece of Dean. He was funny, thoughtful, compassionate, and, hell, everything Ryder wanted in a partner. He'd been perfect, everything he needed. And he'd fallen hard for him. He had wanted a relationship with Dean. Something that would last. And he'd intended to win Dean's heart before he had to deploy again. But that wasn't going to happen now.

His whole life had changed in a moment — he hadn't even had time to blink. He saw it over and over again every time he closed his eyes. Covering Joel as the mine detonated. Sharp metal slicing through his calf and severing it. Then it got fuzzy, there was pain and so much blood. He remembered Bentley yelling for help and applying a tourniquet to his thigh to stop him from bleeding out.

Cursing, he clenched his hand and stared down at the stump where his right leg used to be. The doctors assured him that he was healing well, he'd started rehab and was ready to be fitted for a prosthetic, but what did that matter? His Army career was over, he was going to have to transition to civvy life. And he had no clue what he was going to do. He was a soldier. He didn't want to be anything else.

And worse, he had lost Dean before even getting a chance with him. It wasn't as if he could ask him to be here through this. To wait and remain by his side for the months of him going through rehab with Ryder having little to offer other than being a burden. Plus, lately Dean loved to travel— he deserved someone who could do that with him. The doctors said he could do everything he used to do with the prosthetic but that wasn't true, he couldn't be a soldier now, could he? So he doubted he could go backpacking around Europe either. Maybe he was being pessimistic and negative but he couldn't seem to help but think that everything was ruined. They called him a hero and said he was lucky to be alive so why didn't he feel that way?

He knew he needed Dean. He had always had words of encouragement and support whenever he had been at his lowest. The loneliness was overwhelming him as he reached for the small wooden kangaroo on his bedside table. He wouldn't be giving it to Dean, but he couldn't bear to part with it.

"Is that for me?"

Ryder jumped and gaped as Dean entered his room. He was even more gorgeous than his picture. Well over six feet, Dean was lanky and had a fit body that was highlighted by his tight denim jeans and faded cargo jacket. His jet black hair was cut short, styled to appear tousled. Piercing gray-green eyes stared at him, seeming to draw Ryder into their depths. He saw sadness there but there was joy too. That connection he had felt to Dean sparked and he wished he could get up so he could pull Dean in for a hug to prove he was real and not a dream he'd created. "Dean."

"The one and only," Dean said with that sweet southern drawl of his and an easy smile to match. "How in the world did you manage to find that?"

"I kinda stumbled upon it." Ryder clutched the carving in his hand. It would be too easy to simply talk to Dean and forget all the reasons he wanted him to stay away. But he had to be strong, stay resolved. Dean didn't need a broken man and wouldn't want one either. And he didn't want Dean staying out of pity or a misguided sense of commitment. "What are you doing here? Didn't Ben give you the letter?"

"He did and I decided you were playing a martyr and I don't want you doing that. I'm not going to just walk away when you need someone right now." Dean took a step toward the bed.

Ryder *did* need someone, preferably Dean. Still, he couldn't admit that. "You've done enough. You don't need to put your life on hold for another year waiting on me."

"You're worth the wait." Dean took another step. "You'll recover, and I'll be here to help you get past this."

"There's no recovering!" Ryder angrily threw the covers back and Dean turned white as a sheet. "My leg is gone! It's never going to be the same. I'm not the man you knew. The sooner you accept that the easier it will be for you — for both of us."

Dean's gaze remained fixated on the stump of Ryder's leg, wrapped in a light bandage and sock. "God, Ryder. I'm so sorry."

"Yeah, me too." Ryder deflated as he saw that Dean was slightly shaking. "Look, just go, please. You don't need to be here."

"Why?" Dean's gaze now searched his face. "You are the man I wrote letters to. The one who called me every week, just so I could hear your voice. I told you things that I'd never told anyone else. Not even Dax. You know we connected, you said so yourself. This doesn't change that."

"It does." Ryder drew the covers back around him defensively. "I'm not anything but a burden that I refuse to have you bear. You deserve better than me, Dean."

"That's ridiculous," Dean growled. "You can pull yourself together. Where that's spirit that I lo—I admire? Where's the fight? You can do anything you want. We can, together. Give us a chance."

Ryder focused on the blankets, not meeting Dean's stare.

"There is no us. As for the fight, I guess I lost that when my leg got blown off and my world ripped away."

"This is not the end of the world, damn it!" Dean grabbed his chin, forcing Ryder to meet his gaze, and he gasped as he saw the pain in Dean's eyes. "You're alive. That's what matters to me."

"I wish it mattered to me," Ryder said before he could stop himself.

Dean's eyes widened. He looked as if Ryder had slapped him. He shook Ryder. "You bastard, don't you dare say that! Do you know what I'd give to have Dax back? Do you?" His voice rose. "I know this is awful and I wish to God you'd never been hurt this way, but you're still here and to me that matters. Do you hear me? Before I got here I was sitting in that damn café praying that I hadn't lost you because I wasn't sure I could take it!"

"I'm sorry for saying that. I didn't really mean it," Ryder whispered, realizing that he was lucky to still be here. To have this chance to meet Dean. So what was he doing? Torn between pulling Dean in for a hug or shoving him away, Ryder didn't know what to do. It stunned him that Dean cared so much about him. It shouldn't have but now everything just felt more *real* with them touching. "It's just I'm not a soldier anymore. I have no idea what I'm going to do," he added, voice nearly cracking. "For me it feels like the end of the world. You don't need to hang around here watching me fall apart."

"Tough, I'm not going anywhere." Dean leaned in and wrapped him in an embrace. "I'm here. You can let go."

Being held by Dean felt like coming home, and Ryder relaxed into it. He hadn't felt safe until then and how could he possibly push Dean away when he craved this comfort? Unable to stop himself, he threw his arms around Dean and buried his face in his T-shirt, inhaling the scent of laundry soap and sandalwood. "Damn you, you're supposed to walk away."

"Yeah right," Dean whispered in his hair. "You know me

better than that."

"I can't do a relationship right now. I just can't."

"I'm not asking you to. I just want you to let me help. We're friends, aren't we?" Dean ran a soothing hand down Ryder's back.

"Yeah," Ryder said around a strangled sob.

"So then let me do this for you." Dean kissed the top of Ryder's head and he wished those lips were on his instead. He couldn't commit to anything right now but he could only imagine how good a kiss from Dean would be. "Please, Ryder. I can't leave you hurting like this. It's killing me."

"I'm more scared than I've ever been," Ryder finally admitted after a few moments. "The pain… I swear it feels sometimes like my leg is still there. Then I get angry 'cause it's not."

Dean sank beside him on the bed, drawing Ryder closer but mindful of his leg. "I wish I could do something."

"You're doing exactly what I need you to." Ryder tangled his fingers in Dean's shirt, not wanting to lose the contact that made him feel alive and not so jaded and disconnected. He reached for the kangaroo he had dropped beside them. "Here. This isn't how I wanted to give this to you but, uh—"

Dean pressed a finger to Ryder's lips. "Thanks. I like him." He turned the kangaroo over in his hand, admiring the hand-carved animal. "I'm amazed you managed to find this."

"The guy was amazing at woodcarving. He had all sorts of wooden animals. I saw them, got him to carve one and bartered with some coffee and my watch."

"Your watch?"

"It was a cheap sports one, no big deal." Ryder listened to the steady beat of Dean's heart, the sound lulling him as his tiredness hit him full force. "I'm gonna fall asleep like this."

"You want me to stay then?"

Insecurity filled Ryder again. When was the reality of the situation going to hit Dean and send him running? "If you don't have anywhere you have to be."

"I cleared my plans for the weekend so we could spend it together," Dean replied, making Ryder wish things were different again. A whole weekend with Dean would've been amazing. He'd had plans too for Dean before he was injured, but now, like everything else, he had to change how things were going to go. "I can stay until visiting hours are over today then come back in the morning."

"They're going to release me Monday. I was in the hospital in Germany for nearly a month. I'm so ready to get out of here."

"That's good. Do you have someplace to go?" Ryder could hear the concern in Dean's voice.

"The rehab facility for now. I'll probably be able to find an apartment soon and stay there until my rehab is done."

"Is anyone allowed to go with you to rehab?"

"Yeah, they encourage us to have someone there. But… I don't have anyone. I've been doing the exercises on my own here." He paused, thinking of tomorrow and how he dreaded it. Gathering up courage he added, "I'm, uh, supposed to be fitted tomorrow for the temp prosthetic. Think you could come?"

Dean didn't hesitate. "Just tell me when and where."

Ryder couldn't help but smile as he pulled back so he could see Dean's face. "Thanks, I've been freaking out about it. Gotta learn to walk all over again now that my wound is pretty much healed."

"You'll be up and running in no time," Dean said and Ryder wished he had his optimism.

He shook his head in frustration. "Doc says it's going to let me do everything I used to but I don't believe him."

"Why not?"

"It's not going to let me be a soldier in the field again, is it?" Ryder regretted snapping when Dean flinched.

Dean ran his fingers through Ryder's hair, which he knew was growing quickly. He hadn't cut it and wouldn't need to now. "No, but you're still a soldier. Why can't you be a recruiter, do a desk job, logistics or something like that?"

Bitterness rose up and tasted like bile in Ryder's throat. "Yeah 'cause guys will be lining up to join when they see me."

"You're a hero who sacrificed his leg for his country." Dean's soft voice soothed away the hurt and anger overwhelming Ryder. "I'm proud of you and I know everyone else will be too."

Ryder couldn't speak. To hear those words from Dean meant a great deal. A calmness washed over him and his eyes almost drifted shut.

"You don't have to think about it now. Let's take it one day at a time," Dean continued. Letting go for a moment, he slipped out of his jacket and tossed it toward the nearby chair then toed off his boots. He lay back with Ryder, allowing him to get more comfortable as they stretched out, and Ryder rested his head on Dean's shoulder. "Why don't you rest and later I'll go pick us up something to eat? I'm sure you're sick of the food here."

Ryder chuckled. "Yeah, I am." He was grateful to have Dean there. He'd always been alone, pushing people away because he knew eventually they'd leave. It was the story of his life whenever he cared about someone. He wanted Dean to be different and the comfort he was offering along with the way he was holding him made Ryder believe that maybe he was. "I'm glad you're here, Dean."

"Me too." Dean brushed a kiss to Ryder's temple then froze. "Sorry I— I couldn't help myself."

Ryder met Dean's gaze. The affection in those liquid depths made his heart stutter. "It's okay." He traced his fingers along Dean's clean-shaven jaw. "This kind of feels like a dream."

Dean captured his fingers then pressed a kiss to Ryder's palm. "Yeah, it does." He smiled and for the first time since the injury Ryder felt hopeful that maybe things wouldn't be so bad as long as he had Dean to help him through.

Chapter Twelve

Once Ryder had drifted off Dean relaxed. His gaze traveled over Ryder's six foot frame. His body was lean and hard, the toll of the past month evident. Ryder was tense even in sleep, wound tightly and ready for anything. Dean knew the trust involved for Ryder to be sleeping. Daring to touch, Dean traced his fingertips over Ryder's angled cheekbones, down to his jaw and the dimple in his chin. His sapphire blue eyes were closed over long lashes. Shortly cropped dark brown hair seemed to be wavy now that it was growing. He could imagine running his fingers through it if Ryder didn't decide to cut it.

Dean ran his hand over the starched hospital shirt and forced his eyes farther down to Ryder's leg. He couldn't see much with the blanket in the way, but Ryder had shocked him earlier. It wasn't so much the fact that he was missing his leg, it was the tragedy and miracle wrapped together that had shaken him. So close to losing him before they even met and now everything had changed. Ryder would let him be here as a friend but as to what Dean wanted? He imagined he'd have to find a hell of a way to prove to Ryder that this didn't matter. He'd fallen in love through their letters and phone calls—having met him had simply confirmed those feelings and he wasn't about to let that slip through his fingers.

Even in the state he was in Ryder was handsome and incredibly sexy. Dean couldn't let those thoughts wander because that'd be seriously embarrassing. Though maybe it'd help Ryder see that he was still desirable to Dean. He wanted him, he had for months. And once Ryder was in a better state of mind, he'd pursue him and win him over. He'd never wanted anyone so badly. How had Ryder gotten so deeply under his skin? He couldn't explain it, just like he couldn't explain the connection they'd had, or the way they had seemed fated to meet.

Chewing on his lip, Dean thought of maybe getting up to expel the energy coursing through him but Ryder seemed so peaceful he didn't want to risk waking him. He closed his eyes, needing to think without the temptation of Ryder beside him. It didn't help really. He could still feel the rise and fall of Ryder's chest. Not to mention that he wanted to bury his nose in Ryder's neck and breathe him in. Under the hospital antiseptic there was something that reminded him of a warm, lazy Sunday afternoon curled up with a book on the porch, leaving him content.

A buzzing interrupted his thoughts. It took him a moment but he realized it was from his phone in his jacket. He knew who it was and though he thought it could wait, the last thing he wanted Jessie to do was worry. He tried slipping out of bed but Ryder grabbed his arm.

"Don't go," Ryder said in his sleep.

Dean bent over and kissed Ryder's temple. "I have to get my phone. I won't leave." He gently removed Ryder's hand and waited a moment but he stayed asleep. After he dug his iPhone out of his pocket, he returned Jessie's missed call. He didn't want Ryder to wake so he padded out of the room then thought of something. He turned back and draped his jacket over Ryder. He wondered if his cologne would smell as good as Ryder's did to him.

"Jessie?"

"Sweetie, I didn't interrupt, did I? I just wanted to be sure everything was okay. Last you texted me you thought something was wrong."

He slumped against the wall outside the room. His voice cracked as he replied, "He's hurt bad, Jess. That's why he didn't show."

"Oh my God, how bad?"

"He lost his leg," Dean managed, swallowing the lump in his throat.

"Damn, that's awful. But he'll be all right?" Jessie's voice trembled a bit.

"Yeah, he's got a rough road ahead but..." Dean poked his head in the room. "He's gonna be okay. I'm making sure of that. Even if he's being stubborn."

"Didn't want to be a burden, huh?"

"Yep, you can guess what I said to that." Dean filled her in on parts of their conversation.

Jessie chuckled. "You are a force to be reckoned with lately."

"A lot's changed, so I had to, too."

"I know, I think Dax would be proud."

"I hope so." Dean smiled even though it hurt. "I wish he was here. He'd know what to do, how to help Ryder."

"Just be there for him. He's got to be scared. All you gotta do is show him that you're not going anywhere and the rest will work itself out."

"You're right. Thanks."

"Anytime, sweetie. You let me know if I can do anything, okay?"

"I will." Dean saw a couple headed toward Ryder's room. "Jess, I gotta go. I'll call you back."

"Okay, take care."

Dean disconnected the call and slipped his phone in his pocket. A lanky man was holding the hand of a willowy woman with long black hair and a piercing green gaze. The man had a baby on his hip. The little girl had adorable curls and big brown eyes like her father, though he had a patch covering one side of his face.

"Hello," he greeted, wondering if they were Ryder's friends.

"Hi, I'm Joel." The man held out his hand. "My wife, Lucy, and our little one, Amelia."

"I'm Dean." Dean shook the offered hand and smiled. "It's nice to meet you. You have the cutest daughter."

Joel beamed with pride. "Yes, we do."

Lucy brushed her hair back. "We're here to see Ryder. Joel's been waiting to thank him."

"He saved my life, brought me home to my family." Joel hugged his wife. "Is he up for visitors?"

"He's resting but let me go talk to him."

"Thank you."

Dean nodded and went in to gently shake Ryder awake. He thought it'd be good for Ryder's spirits to see the man whose life he had saved. Remind him of the good he did. "Ry, your buddy Joel is here with his family and wants to come in."

Scrubbing a hand over his face, Ryder sat up. "Really? How is he?"

"Patch over his eye. But he seems fine. He says you saved his life."

Ryder ducked his head. "He has a baby. I had to get him home, he was my man. My responsibility."

"And you got him home." Dean pressed a kiss to Ryder's temple. "Want me to let them in?"

"Could you...help me into the chair over there? I don't want to lie in bed when they're visiting."

"Sure, what do you need?"

"Just a hand."

Dean couldn't help it, he held out his hand. "All yours," he purred. "What do you want me to do with it?"

"Well, we have company so I'll tell you later." Ryder laughed, took his hand and moved so he had his leg hanging over the side of the bed. Dean helped him up, then supported Ryder as he hopped the few feet to the chair. He helped Ryder sink down, relishing the hold he had on him. He ran a hand down Ryder's side before stepping away.

Ryder nodded and Dean let Joel and his family in. Lucy began crying as she hugged Ryder, repeatedly thanking him over and over. Joel gave him a one-armed hug as well and Dean watched as Amelia ended up sitting in Ryder's lap, happily cooing as he tickled her chin.

Not wanting to intrude, Dean sat quietly on the windowsill.

Joel took a seat beside Ryder, and Lucy wrapped her arms around her husband from behind. "I'm so sorry, Ryder," Joel apologized. "If I hadn't been so stupid…"

Dean wasn't surprised when Ryder said, "Don't be. It wasn't your fault. Any one of us could've stepped on that mine. You listened and you stayed calm, that's what counts. I'm just glad we both got out of there."

"Me too." Joel smiled at Amelia. "Thank you for getting me home."

"You're welcome." Ryder let Amelia grab his finger. She was just the cutest thing. Dean saw Ryder smile at her and hoped it clicked that he'd done a good thing here. Ryder's attention returned to Joel. "How's your eye?"

"Likely I won't be able to see out of it. They're probably going to give me a medical discharge. I'm relieved, to be honest, I don't ever want to go back," Joel told him.

"He's going back to school to finish getting his law degree." Lucy kissed the top of Joel's head. "We got it all figured out, don't we, *mi amor*?"

"Yeah we do. What about you, Ryder?"

"Not sure yet. I still got a lot to figure out," Ryder admitted. "But I've got Dean with me now so it'll work itself out." He smiled at Dean and his heart thudded.

"I hear you. Life is good as long as I have my girls." Joel grinned. "Maybe you could get a degree in architecture? All those sketches you drew of the buildings around us were incredible."

"That's not a bad idea," Ryder agreed.

"Are you going to be released soon?" Lucy asked.

"Yeah, on Monday."

"Where are you staying?"

"Either the rehab facility or—"

"With me," Dean added, before he could stop himself. "I've got a spare room and it'll take a while to get an apartment and you don't need to stay in that facility. You could stay with me... If you want," he hastily added, feeling himself redden as all eyes were now on him.

Ryder's gaze softened. "If you're sure it's no trouble."

"Not at all." Dean just wanted Ryder to himself. Wanted him close. Wanted to know he was here, alive, safe. He didn't want him going anywhere else.

"Well, then I'm staying with Dean," Ryder told Joel and Lucy.

"You're both welcome, anytime," Dean added.

"Thank you." Joel tilted his head. "Looks like I won the pool."

"Pool?" Ryder asked.

"Uh, yeah, the guys all saw how happy you were before it all went to crap. Some thought you were getting promoted, others thought you were just glad to get outta there. Me, I thought you had met someone."

"I'd have talked about Dean more but you know how Hicks is," Ryder grumbled. "Bigoted SOB."

"Yeah, another reason I'm glad I'm not going back," Joel said.

"If you don't mind, how long have you been together?" Lucy asked.

"Oh well." Dean wasn't sure how to answer. "We were pen pals for a year."

"We just met today," Ryder added. "We had plans but this kind of threw a wrench in them... And I didn't want to—"

Dean moved so he was kneeling beside Ryder. "We're not together yet, Lucy," he admitted. "But..." He put his hand over Ryder's. "I'm hoping to change that."

Ryder locked gazes with him. "So am I."

"*Mi corazón*, don't they remind you of us when we first met?" Lucy asked as she hugged Joel.

"*Si*." Joel scooped up Amelia as she fussed and held out her little hands to him. "We don't want to intrude. We can come back."

"Amelia is getting hungry anyway," Lucy agreed.

"I really appreciate you coming by." Ryder bumped fists with Joel. "We should do dinner sometime. Hang out."

"Yeah, let's do that. It was nice meeting you, Dean."

"Likewise."

Joel passed Amelia to Lucy who said, "Take care. Let us know if you need anything."

"I will, thanks."

Chapter Thirteen

When they were alone again, Dean was immediately by his side, an apologetic look on his face. "Gosh, Ry. I'm real sorry, I didn't mean to put any pressure on you. I just hated the thought of you stuck in another type of hospital and I thought maybe they were gonna offer you a place to stay and I just blurted it out because I wanted you with me. You don't have to stay at my place, I know you wanted to take things slow and I'm not pushing, I just—"

Ryder pressed a finger to Dean's lips. "Whoa, are you always this articulate?" he joked.

"Usually, yeah." Dean blushed a deep shade of red.

With a shake of his head, Ryder traced his fingers over Dean's cheek. "You didn't pressure me. You were right about all the stuff you said. We can still take things slow..." Oh hell, who was he kidding? Why was he denying what they both wanted? The urge to kiss Dean as he gazed at him was overwhelming. "Or maybe not..."

Insecure but daring to take a risk, Ryder decided to see how Dean would react. He dipped down and pressed his lips to Dean's. With a gasp, Dean's lips parted for him and Ryder tugged him up. Tongues tangled and teeth clashed as a hunger took over. Dean's taste, his kisses, the feel of him made Ryder crazy. Straddling his good leg, Dean then sank onto it. They broke for a breath but then Dean dove back in for more. His tongue hit the hotspot on the roof of Ryder's mouth and he moaned. He roamed his hands over Dean's sides, feeling strong muscles under soft cotton. For the first time in a long time arousal filled him.

Lust-filled eyes met his and Ryder gasped out loud. *He*

wants me, like this. God I'm stupid if I push him away. There was an obvious bulge in Dean's jeans and he was scrabbling to get closer to Ryder, not away. Ryder couldn't believe that, still happiness bubbled up and his confidence started returning. Maybe he could be what Dean needed. So why wait? They hadn't planned to.

Dean kissed along his stubble-covered jaw, one of his hands fisted in Ryder's shirt. "Oh, God." He nipped Ryder's neck and Ryder tipped his head back, giving him better access. "We gotta stop before I can't."

Massaging Dean's ass through his jeans, Ryder wasn't sure he wanted to stop. But Dean deserved more than this, here in a hospital. He wanted to make love to him, to have it be somewhere they could spend as much time as they wanted, exploring and learning each other's bodies. Ryder wanted to know every inch of Dean, wanted to know what made him moan, beg, and gasp. Still, his hands had a mind of their own.

"Damn, Ry," Dean breathed, grinding against him. "Do you know how many nights I dreamed of this?"

"As many as I did," Ryder answered, locking gazes with Dean. He cupped Dean's cheek and kissed him gently. "And, man, was that hell 'cause I had no privacy and blue balls."

Dean trailed his fingers down Ryder's stomach toward the tent in his sleep pants. His cock jumped as Dean's hand brushed against it, and he wished there wasn't a cloth barrier. "Well, I'm not sure about privacy but I can make certain you're taken care of. I do believe you asked for a hand?"

Ryder knew they shouldn't. Anyone could walk in. But logic had fled in the wake of his need for Dean. Since his injury he'd been depressed, angry and ready to throw in the towel. He felt so alive and grateful to be in this moment. Why deny what they'd both wanted for almost a year? There were no longer oceans between them, preventing them from acting on their desire. Ryder finally had Dean in his arms, right where he wanted him. Screw it, he had to have Dean. *Now*.

He grabbed the back of Dean's head and pulled him in for another hungry kiss. Dean tugged on the drawstring, and he somehow managed to get the pants down enough for Ryder's cock to spring free. He groaned as it filled, hitting his belly and smearing a drop of pre-cum. He almost came when Dean dragged his finger through it and broke the kiss to suck on the digit. He popped the button on Dean's jeans, yanking down the zipper. It took Dean lifting himself up and Ryder helping as he got his jeans down enough along with his boxers to release Dean's dick from its confines. It was long and slightly curved—Ryder moaned out loud at the sight. He wished he could strip Dean of all his clothes but for now this would have to do. Though he knew they likely didn't have much time, he had to slow it down just a little, enjoy this. He'd dreamed of it often enough, but now that it was real he wanted to take it all in.

He leaned forward and latched his mouth on Dean's nipple through his cotton shirt, sucking on it. Dean gasped and gripped his shoulders. He whimpered when Ryder nipped it. "Like that?" He blew lightly over the hardened nub, watching as Dean shuddered with desire before giving the other nipple the same attention.

"More please," Dean pleaded.

He snuck his hands under Dean's shirt, caressing all over. He slowly made his way to Dean's firm ass, squeezing. Dean threw his head back, sexily riding Ryder's thigh as he sought some type of relief.

Ryder felt his need, he wrapped his fingers around Dean's cock. He loved the feel of the velvety hardness. "Hell yeah," Ryder breathed. He stroked from the base to the tip, using the pre-cum to smooth his stroking. He thumbed the slit and Dean actually cried out.

"Shh, baby," he urged. "We don't want to get interrupted."

"Sorry, I just...wanted this for so long. Need you so much." Dean pushed into Ryder's hand as they locked gazes. His eyes were now dark with arousal, pupils dilated. His lips were kiss-swollen, skin glistening with sweat, and body pliant in Ryder's hands—he was breathtaking.

"I know, I know," Ryder agreed, nipping Dean's lips. He sped up, pumping Dean rapidly. Dean's hips rocked erratically as his orgasm overtook him after just a few more strokes. He bit down on Ryder's shoulder, his back arching as he came, spilling his release into Ryder's hand and onto his own aching cock. He was so close himself but right now he was loving how hard he'd made Dean come.

"Jesus, Ry. That was amazing." With a sated smile, Dean rested his head on Ryder's shoulder.

Ryder wanted a taste. He lifted his hand, licking his fingers clean as he tasted Dean for the first time. He gasped in surprise when Dean's lips crashed against his. He moaned into Dean's mouth as Dean took him in hand, he was desperate for Dean's touch.

"Oh I know what *I* want." Dean pulled back and before Ryder blinked he was on his knees before him, spreading Ryder's thighs. He didn't even have a chance to think about not wanting Dean down there to see his leg because Dean just caressed his skin, making him forget everything except that he wanted Dean's mouth on him.

"Please," he begged, grasping Dean's head. "Oh please."

Dean planted a trail of kisses down Ryder's cock from the root to the tip, before taking the head in his mouth and licking the slit, tasting Ryder.

"So good," Dean said in a husky voice. He gently slid Ryder down his seat and Ryder spread out as far as the chair would allow, wantonly exposing himself to Dean's ministrations.

"Don't tease, baby. I'm so close."

"Not teasing, enjoying you." Dean grinned then deep-throated Ryder, and to avoid screaming out in pleasure, Ryder bit his lip so hard it nearly bled. He tangled his hands in the short strands of his lover's hair. Dean gripped Ryder's hips, sucking gently as Ryder began thrusting.

Unable to cry out like he wanted because it felt so damn good, Ryder threw his head back, screwing his eyes shut in ecstasy. He lost himself in the sensation of Dean's gorgeous mouth surrounding his heat. He tugged and caressed Dean's hair, letting him know how amazing it felt while his body shuddered and moved on its own accord. The rush of finally having Dean on his knees was hurtling him to the edge far quicker than he'd admit, but he didn't care because Dean had made all coherent thought flee the moment he went down on him.

Ryder twisted his fingers in Dean's hair urging him to go faster. Dean silently hummed, increasing the pace and relaxing his throat, allowing Ryder to thrust harder. Within moments, he was biting on his fist as he fought back moans and cries, it felt so damn good. Reaching into Ryder's sleep pants, Dean then cupped and lightly stroked his balls.

Ryder couldn't hold back anymore. He met Dean's gaze and whispered, "Gonna come!" giving him the chance to pull back. Dean just sucked harder, taking Ryder all the way down until his nose was buried in Ryder's groin. That was his undoing. He pushed upward once more into Dean's mouth as he came, pulsing deeply into his lover's throat in blistering waves that drained him. He enjoyed the sensation of Dean swallowing his release and sucking him completely dry.

"Dean, Dean..." Ryder panted, sinking back into the chair. Sated and content, he basked in his orgasm. Dean released Ryder's softened cock with a wet pop, then licked him clean. Ryder tugged him back into his arms, as he kissed Dean deeply. "That was fucking amazing."

"Yeah, I wish we had time for more." Dean snuggled close. "Gotta make all those dreams come true."

"Hell yeah. My favorite one I always had was you sneaking into the tent and riding me."

Dean took his hand, twining their fingers together. "Mine was you coming home and nailing me to the mattress as you held my hands over my head."

"Damn, I'm going to be screwed if you keep talking like that."

Dean chuckled. "You'll be out of here in no time. Then we can spend a week in bed if you want."

Pressing a kiss to Dean's temple, Ryder said, "Now that's a plan!"

"Are there washcloths in the bathroom?" Dean asked after a few minutes of peaceful quiet. "We should clean up before a nurse comes in."

"Yeah, should be. Could you get me a clean shirt in the drawer too?"

"Sure, babe." Dean kissed him before getting up. He tugged up his boxers, tucked himself back in then buttoned his jeans. His shirt was wrinkled but he just smoothed it out. He then got a shirt and washcloth. Ryder cleaned himself up, changed and had Dean help him up. The chair wasn't comfortable for too long and he didn't want his leg to cramp. He sat back on the bed, amazed at what had just happened. Dean had been all over him. He'd been so scared that he was a turn-off now with his missing leg, but Dean hadn't flinched or hesitated in loving him. He truly had hope now that what he wanted with Dean was possible. And there was no denying that he was in love with him.

"What is it?" Dean placed one of his legs under him and sat opposite Ryder on the mattress. "You're thinking too hard."

"I... The reason I said we should go slow was because I was afraid you wouldn't be attracted to me because of this," Ryder gestured to his leg, "but you just... No one has ever made me feel that good and I forgot there was anything wrong with me."

Dean tilted up Ryder's chin. "There's *nothing* wrong with you. Not to me. And I know you, Ry. It's not just your body I want—though it's sexy as hell. I want *you*. Just like this. Because you're beautiful to me," he confessed and Ryder swore he fell in love all over again at the tender words.

"How did I ever get so lucky?" he asked out loud. Dean

broke into a smile as Ryder took his hand. "I... I'm falling hard for you again right now, Dean," he confessed. "I'm scared because I've never cared or had a relationship last, but with you it just feels right. I want to be with you, I want this."

"Good, then we're on the same page." Dean kissed his palm. "Because I've been falling for you for a while now."

Ryder pulled him over for a tender kiss, wondering if he could get discharged earlier. So he could leave with Dean.

Chapter Fourteen

Dean stayed until visiting hours were over. He'd run and got them dinner then they'd talked for hours, their easy companionship just as comfortable as it'd been while talking on the phone and writing back and forth every chance they got. They'd laughed, flirted and teased. Dean caught Ryder up on the things he'd done in the past few weeks. He helped Ryder plan to look into architecture design. They'd kissed and had a heavy make-out session before Dean had to go. The nurse had given him a few pointed looks on his way out but he didn't care. He didn't want to leave Ryder alone, though he knew there wasn't another option until he was discharged Monday.

Before heading home he made a stop at the hardware store. He had some materials he needed to buy to get the house ready for Ryder. He got everything he needed, then drove home. Jessie had already stopped by to take the dogs out for him—he saw the note and was grateful. Sassy and Bones still went crazy as he stepped through the door. Sassy jumped into his arms and Bones pawed him. He greeted them both then made them sit.

"You both are going to have to be better behaved than this," he chided. "I can't have Ryder falling over because you two are crazy when I come home. C'mon." They followed him to the kitchen where he fed them then let them out.

Once they were taken care of, he grabbed a sweater, some worn gloves and safety goggles. His first repair was the rickety rail on the porch. Dax had taught him all he knew about fixing things up around the house. With a hammer, nails, some two by fours, and sweat he made certain that the rail was as sturdy as could be. He tested it out, pleased when he could put his full weight on it and the posts didn't budge.

That done, he moved into the warm house. Bones and Sassy followed him as he rearranged his living room furniture so it was spread out and there was more room to maneuver. There were small rugs in the kitchen that he taped down. Next stop was the guest bathroom. He put a handrail next to the toilet and a bar in the shower to hold onto. He thought the lip of the shower could be lowered but that'd take more expertise than he had, so he'd have to look into it. He did the same things in his bathroom. It didn't take him long and he was happy with the results. He'd wanted it all done before Ryder came home. He didn't want him to have to ask or worry about it. This way it was all taken care of and Ryder could be safe here. Dean knew one of the biggest risks while Ryder was recovering was having him fall. But he wasn't about to let that happen.

He'd told Ryder he could have the spare room so he made sure it was tidied up and there was plenty of space. Though he secretly hoped that Ryder would want to stay with him. He knew it was a little crazy how fast things had moved but not really. He'd been hoping for months that as soon as Ryder came home they could finally take their relationship to an intimate level. They'd talked for almost a year, bonded, and now today they'd connected with not just their minds and hearts but bodies too. Dean had loved every second. He hadn't thought twice about not acting on his need for Ryder, he'd just given in to what felt right and loved him. He knew it was the right thing, too, because Ryder had been so happy and come alive, his spark returning as Dean had shown him how beautiful he was to him. And damn if he didn't miss him now.

He got ready for bed, and Sassy joined him once he was settled, curling up at his feet. Bones lay in his dog bed in the corner and Dean turned off the lights. His phone rang on the nightstand. *Ryder.*

"Hey, baby. You weren't sleeping were you?" Ryder asked.

"Not yet. What about you, I thought you were going to get some rest?"

"I'm going to try. It's tough... Nightmares," Ryder confessed in a quiet voice. "I just wanted to call and say goodnight."

Dean cradled the phone to his ear as he pulled the covers around him. "How about we talk until we fall asleep? And if you need me later just call, 'kay?"

"I don't want to keep you up."

"You're not. This way we might both get rest."

Dean could hear Ryder smiling. "I'm learning it's best to just do what you say."

"Smart man. So, tell me what you want for breakfast? Oh! There's a great pancake house I know of..."

* * * *

Elena ran through the basics as she showed Ryder how to put on the sock and the temporary prosthetic leg that was fitted with one of his sneakers. She made sure the sock was comfortable and not rubbing, making notes as they went along and telling him adjustments could easily be made. He'd get another one in a few months when his leg stabilized in size and shape. Right now it was about utilizing this and getting him walking again. She had him stand and he mentioned a little discomfort but an adjustment fixed it. She then helped him to a set of bars.

"All right, Ryder. I want you to start here at this end with me and walk to Dean. Take your time. If you need to stop just say so. You've been doing great with the exercises so I know you can do this," Elena, his therapist, encouraged. "Oh and if anything hurts or is uncomfortable tell me so I can fix it, 'kay?"

"Sure thing."

Ryder gripped the two bars tight, nervousness bubbling up. There wasn't much distance between him and Dean but could he make it that far? What if he fell? Or the prosthetic didn't support him? Doubt crept up.

Suddenly, to his surprise, Dean was there, hands drifting to his waist. He leaned in to whisper, "Walk to me, Ry. And I promise when we get out of here, I'll kiss you. Long and slow. Think about that." He squeezed Ryder's hip then moved back to his spot. A big grin split his face and he gave Ryder a come hither gesture.

Damn, if his nerves didn't disappear. Now all he could think about was getting to Dean for that kiss. He glanced back at Elena but she just giggled and watched expectantly.

He honestly didn't think he was attractive in hospital scrubs and wearing a prosthetic but the way Dean was looking at him made him realize again that maybe none of that mattered to Dean. But it mattered to him, and the fact that Dean saw past it made him feel so lucky that Dean had stayed yesterday and given him hope. His life wasn't over. It was just beginning if he embraced this second chance and Dean.

Steeling himself, he took a step forward. He didn't fall. He was supported and it didn't go horribly wrong. The prosthetic was actually comfortable. Maybe it wouldn't be so bad after all. He took another step. And another. Then stopped to take a deep breath. It was difficult but he could do it. Another few steps and before he knew it he had reached Dean.

Shaking slightly, he pulled Dean toward him and decided to screw it and kiss him now. Just a brief kiss because he wasn't sure he'd stop if he deepened it. He hadn't been able to yesterday after all. Featherlight, Ryder brushed his lips against Dean's. It was enough to send him flying once more.

"Thank you," he whispered to Dean. With a smile and feeling like he could do this, he turned around.

"Anytime." Dean leaned in from behind him. "No kissing her. That's only for me."

Laughing, Ryder turned his head. "I'll just have to hurry back for another one then."

"You do that."

Elena was smiling as he walked to her. "Excellent, Ryder. How does it feel?"

"Surprisingly good."

"No pain?"

"Not since you adjusted it." Ryder stopped in front of her. He was a bit tired but he wanted to at least do it a few more times—it was about perseverance and mind over matter. He pointed to his thigh. "There's some pressure here."

Elena made a note and again adjusted a strap. "Better or worse?"

"Better, thanks. Can I go again?"

"Yep, just don't overdo it. I'll have you rest in a few."

"And then?"

"Once you get this down we'll tackle steps. I'll have all sorts of fun stuff for you to do in the upcoming months."

Ryder bit his lip. "Do you think once I get the final fitting I could travel? You know hikes, exploring through old buildings and stuff like that?"

"Ry," Dean interrupted.

"No, we made those plans together. If I can be ready by then I want us to take our trip." Ryder glanced over at Dean. They'd made plans in their letters to visit a cabin resort in the winter and take a hiking trip next summer.

"Oh yeah, no problem. It's all about you, Ryder," Elena told him. "You want to do it you can. I've had people with two prosthetic legs riding bikes and hiking. The only one who can limit you is *you*."

"I'm getting that now," he admitted.

"It's all about the right motivation too. I'm glad you've found yours." Elena winked at him.

"I am too." Ryder turned back to Dean with a smile. He could take on anything knowing that Dean would catch him before he fell. With that thought in mind, he took another step forward.

Chapter Fifteen

Dean pulled his car into the drive, giving Ryder his first view of his home. It was a one story — which meant no stairs to tackle, thank goodness — cottage style home with earth tones and painted trim. Fenced in with a porch. It was cozy. Ryder opened the passenger door and took the crutch Dean handed him after he'd run around to help.

"Nice place."

"Thanks. I'm sorry there's two small steps on the porch." Dean waited by his side. He didn't offer help but Ryder knew he'd give it. He appreciated Dean letting him do this on his own.

He supported himself on the crutch. It was mainly to make sure he didn't lose his balance until he could walk better with the prosthetic. "No biggie. We can take 'em."

Dean grinned and shut the door for Ryder. They made their way slowly to the porch. Ryder could see fresh paint on the rails. "The rail was loose," Dean explained. "Did a little fixing up the other night."

Ryder was touched that Dean had done that for him. Dean stood behind him as he summoned his strength and tackled one step then the other with a whoop of joy.

Dean kissed him before pulling out his house keys. "Let me put the two terrors out back. Sassy has a bad habit of jumping when I first get home."

With a chuckle, Ryder nodded as Dean slipped inside. He heard commotion, laughter then another door opening and closing before footsteps returned. Ryder pushed open the door and stepped inside the entry hall.

"Want the grand tour?" Dean asked. "Oh, I gotta get your

bags in."

"No rush, I want to see the house first."

Dean led him to the spacious living room. A long sofa sat across the room from a flat-screen TV mounted on the wall. Two overstuffed reading chairs bracketed the stone fireplace while a large bay window offered a beautiful view of the street. Bookshelves, overflowing with books, lined the remaining walls.

"I like it." Ryder followed Dean to the kitchen and dining room. An oak table was nestled by two large sliding glass doors. Sassy and Bones waited on the back porch, their tails wagging. Sassy pleaded to be let in as she jumped up and down. A swing sat on the back porch along with a barbecue. Ryder spotted a pool — he put that on the list of things he'd have to learn to do again.

Dean was smiling at his dogs. "You know you can't come in yet, go play!"

The look Sassy gave him had Ryder clutching his sides. "Oh you weren't kidding. She's a diva."

"I spoil her rotten so I suppose I'm to blame." Dean shrugged. "She's a good dog."

Ryder pulled out a chair. "Let her in." He took a seat. He had to win the dog over because he knew she was important to Dean.

Rubbing the back of his head, Dean said, "She might get skittish or nip as a warning. She bit Dax once. She's, uh, real protective of me."

"So a test then." Ryder winked.

Dean pulled open the door, instructing Bones to stay and scooping up Sassy who tried covering him in kisses. "Okay, Sassy. We've had this talk, be nice." He blushed. "Oh gosh, you think I'm a crazy guy who talks to his dog now."

"Why wouldn't you? Dogs are great listeners," Ryder replied. "And I know they understand us on some level." He held out his fist as Dean approached. Sassy growled a little but her tail wagged. He took it as a good sign. He rubbed her ears and got a lick to his hand. So far, so good.

To his surprise she wiggled out of Dean's arms and jumped onto his lap.

She stared up at him, assessing him it seemed. He petted her. "Hey, pretty girl."

She tilted her head then stood, paws on his chest and tried to lick him. He laughed and so did Dean. She nuzzled his hand then leaped off, returning with a tattered chew toy.

"Piece of cake." Ryder took the stuffed lion and threw it.

Dean planted his butt against the table. "That was amazing. She's never taken to anyone like that."

Sassy brought him the toy and he tossed it again. "I love dogs. Maybe she senses it."

"Or she knows how I feel," Dean said aloud then ducked his head.

Heart thudding, Ryder managed to get to his feet again. He didn't know what to say. Was it too soon to say he loved Dean? "What we feel," he corrected softly, leaning over for a kiss.

Dean then showed him the guest bathroom and bedroom. Again Ryder was amazed at the little touches Dean had obviously added to accommodate him but made like it was nothing. To Ryder it was—he'd known he was going to have to ask for them but his stubborn pride hadn't let him. Dean had gone and taken care of it, saving his pride and taking care of him all at once. He fell in love just a little harder when he saw that the same had been done in the master bathroom.

Dean's room was just as cozy and lived in as the rest of the house. Navy blue walls matched the bed's comforter and pillows. Two dressers and a bookshelf made up the rest of the furniture and the recessed window framed a window seat.

"I cleared out some closet and drawer space just in case." Dean ran a hand through his hair. "Um, I didn't know if you wanted to or not, but you can stay here with me in my room or you can have your own..."

Dean wanted him here. Damn, when had he ever had a

real home? Never. And yet here Dean was offering, making him feel wanted and safe. He blinked a couple of times, feeling his eyes moisten.

Ryder swallowed the lump in his throat. "I'd like to be with you," he managed. Maybe he'd sleep tonight—he felt comfortable with Dean, protected. As if his nightmares wouldn't haunt him.

"Are you okay?" Dean asked. "Need a pain pill?"

"No, no. It's not that." Ryder sank onto the silk sheets.

"Did I do something?" Insecurity filled Dean's eyes.

"Only good things." He patted the space beside him and Dean sat. "Thank you," he whispered.

"For what?"

"All the little things you did so I could be comfortable so it could feel like home to me." Ryder paused. "I've never had a home, Dean. Just temporary ones like I told you. That'd I pass through and have to move on." He glanced around, imagining adding his touches, having his stuff lying around. He could see it. His watch next to Dean's on the dresser, a picture of them on the nightstand, his shoes by the door...

Drawing him into his arms, Dean then kissed Ryder's shoulder. "I know. No more temporary homes, babe."

"No," he agreed. *I think this is where I belong.* He turned his head so he could press his lips to Dean's. He couldn't put into words what this meant but maybe he could show him.

There was a knock at the front door before it opened. Dean groaned. "Looks like Mama has decided to stop by." He gave Ryder an apologetic look. "You up for it? She means well, I promise. But I can ask her to come by and see you later."

"Nah, she's here. Let's go say hi." Truthfully he was nervous—he'd never met another guy's family before but he knew Dean was close to his mom and that she was a big part of his life. He only hoped she liked him.

Ryder seemed as nervous as Dean felt as they went into

the living room. He hadn't told his mama yet about Ryder moving in. It was going to be a shock, he knew, but in his heart Dean believed it was the right decision.

His mama smiled and stepped toward Ryder, giving him a hug and a kiss on the cheek. "Hello, Ryder. It's nice to finally meet you after hearing so much about you."

"Only good things I hope." Ryder winked, and she chuckled.

"Yes, look at you. Are you hungry? I know how those hospitals are so I brought over a pan of my lasagna."

"Well, that was kind of you." Ryder smiled. "I'd like to try some."

"C'mon then, we can talk and eat." His mama turned her attention to him. "Sweetheart, don't just stand there. Where's my hello?"

Shaking his head, Dean gave her a big hug. "Hi, Mama. Thanks for stopping by."

"I hadn't heard from you so I called Jessie and I figured Ryder could use some good comfort food."

"You're the best." Dean kissed her cheek and they went into the dining room. His mama insisted on serving them, though Dean and Ryder both tried to help. She sat down when they all had food and got to know Ryder. Before Dean knew it they were all laughing and having a good time just talking.

That was until his mom asked, "So are you staying close by?"

Crap. Confusion filled Ryder's face so Dean answered, "No, Ryder lived in the barracks. And I didn't want him staying in the hospital any longer than he had to." He put his hand over Ryder's, resting on the table. "So, he's staying here."

"Oh." She raised an eyebrow and seemed to be speechless, which he'd never seen before. Then again he hadn't ever been so serious as to move in a guy before either. "Well, you do have the spare room."

Should he pick his battles or be honest? Ryder shared

a look with him, letting Dean decide how to respond. He could let it slide. But he didn't want to hurt Ryder. "Mama, you know Ry and I are together."

She glanced at their joined hands. "Of course I do. If this is what you both want you know I'll support you, Dean. I trust you but, Ryder, you'd best not hurt my son."

"No, ma'am." Ryder cleared his throat. "You've been kind not bringing up the elephant in the room but I'll tell you I was in a real bad way because of my leg. And then Dean…" Ryder locked gazes with him. "He made me realize how lucky I am to still be here."

His mama broke into a smile. "Please, all of Dean's friends call me Mama Beth and since you're more than a friend you're welcome to."

"I…" Ryder blinked and stared down at his plate. "Thank you."

His mama seemed concerned. "Did I say something?"

"No, not at all. I just… I'm a foster kid. Not once did I ever get to call anyone Mom," Ryder admitted.

His mama leaned toward Ryder and took his free hand. "You can ask Dean—I take people under my wings all the time, so to speak. I like taking care of others. It's a blessing I've gotten Dean as a son. And you'll see you'll be a part of our family in no time. Anything you need you just ask. I'm here for you. And I'm proud as hell of you for the sacrifice you made. My Dax made one too. I just wish he had made it home. I'm glad you did and that you know it's a gift. Because every day is one, so go on, you two, and make the most of it." She squeezed Ryder's hand. "All right?"

Ryder nodded then softly said, "Yes, Mama."

Dean smiled at his mama. He knew she would love Ryder as soon as she got to know him. Just like he had. And he knew she'd want to nurture him and help him get through this, she was so good at that. They'd help Ryder get on his feet in no time. "Mama's right," he agreed. "It's a blessing."

Chapter Sixteen

The next day Dean had to work. He'd called in sick the day before so Ryder could get settled and he appreciated it but he didn't want him missing any more days. His students needed their teacher. And he could get by on his own. Beth had offered to drive him to his therapy and afterward he had spent the afternoon unpacking his few belongings and simply enjoying the peace and quiet. Sassy, his newest shadow, followed him throughout the house He watched Netflix, catching up on his favorite shows. He enrolled in classes at Fayetteville for the fall semester. His goal was to get a degree, then maybe start his own architecture firm. He did need to brush up on his skills so he planned on sitting outside and drawing the next day. Right now he wanted to try to start dinner before Dean came home, to surprise him and pull his weight around here.

Stuffed chicken marsala and mashed potatoes were Dean's favorites and Ryder was glad to find all the ingredients needed in the fridge. He grabbed a stool and sat, preparing the chicken at the island and standing for a bit at a time. When the chicken was stuffed, coated and put in a pan, he managed to slip it in the oven. He sautéed onions and mushrooms in a wine sauce and had the potatoes boiling in a pot. He'd forgotten he enjoyed cooking. It was nice picking out the food he wanted to eat and enjoy. No ready-made meal or hospital crap.

His phone rang and he answered it without looking, thinking it was Dean calling to tell him he was on his way home. He was relieved he didn't get a chance to say 'Hey, baby' as Bentley talked first. "Hey, man, I thought you were getting released today so I came by but you're already gone."

"Actually, they discharged me yesterday. I'm here at Dean's." Ryder leaned against the counter, taking the weight off his leg.

"Really? So you two worked things out?" Why the hell did Bentley sound disappointed?

"Yeah, I'm glad you told him where I was. Turns out he was just what I needed to pull myself up from rock bottom."

"Hmm, just be careful. You just met."

"I've known him for almost a year, Ben. He's been there for me. He knows more than I've even told you so I'd appreciate you trusting me and actually sounding happy," he snapped. "You were a real jerk acting disgusted just because I'm injured, by the way."

"Whoa, no need to blow up at me," Bentley replied. "I didn't, it just takes some getting used to is all. It's just, I was there. I..."

"Dean didn't need to take any time, so think on that one." Ryder disconnected the call. Bentley had a bad habit of riling him up. He was in a good mood, feeling happier than he had in a long time. No way was Bentley going to ruin that or bring him down so that he was miserable too. He ignored the phone twice when Bentley tried to call him back.

Dinner was almost finished when Dean came through the door. The dogs greeted him and Ryder poured two glasses of wine, holding one out as Dean entered the kitchen.

"Welcome home, baby. Dinner will be ready in five."

"It smells delicious." Dean took the glass but set it aside, cupping Ryder's face and kissing him deeply. Ryder melted into it, loving how Dean made him feel. "Thank you, I really like this. Coming home to you, I mean."

Ryder grinned. "I'm going to spoil you with my cooking."

"Yes, please!" Dean chuckled and gave Ryder his glass. "To us."

"To us," Ryder toasted, sharing a sip.

"How was your day?" Dean asked, pulling plates from the cupboard as Ryder told him what he'd done. Dean then shared his day. They moved around one another effortlessly as if they'd been doing it all along. Ryder set the table, as Dean brought in the food. They each helped themselves and dug in. Ryder was a bit tired but Dean had two helpings and praised the meal so it was well worth it.

* * * *

Dean could tell that Ryder was exhausted from his increased activity. He might have overdone it a little but he was proud of him and relieved he was in a better mindset. He pulled Ryder up from the sofa where they'd been watching a movie and led him to bed. Ryder sank down and he started to remove his prosthesis.

"Let me." Dean knelt in front of his lover and removed the limb. It didn't bother him, it made him sad, but he hid that because he knew Ryder was fighting depression. Still, the best way he thought he could help was proving to Ryder that he could handle it. Ryder could lean on him and he'd take care of him. He rested the appendage against the nightstand. "Soap and water, yeah?"

With a tender look, Ryder just nodded. He removed the compression sock and Dean washed it with mild soap and water in the bathroom sink, then wrapped it in a towel to dry. He got a bowl of soap and water and went back to Ryder. Gently he inspected the limb—the scar had healed nicely, though he knew it would take up to a year to heal on the inside. He'd done some research in the library. He didn't like being in the dark, he wanted to know all he could. Seeing no redness or swelling, he dipped a washcloth in the water and washed the residual limb carefully, keeping his touch light against Ryder's skin.

Dean could feel Ryder's intense gaze. He knew he had hang-ups, understandably. But to him Ryder was no less attractive. He loved him for who he was, that was all there was to it. His soldier had made a sacrifice, one he'd see every day and be grateful that Ryder was in his life despite it all. It showed his courage, his caring for others, his loyalty, all the traits that he loved in his partner.

"How's it feel?"

"Like I did a lot today but not bad." Ryder chewed on his lip.

"What is it?"

"Nothing..."

"Ry?"

"I should've called you..." Ryder put his hand over Dean's, stopping him for a moment. "When I first got home, I mean. Or, hell, even at the hospital in Germany. I shouldn't have waited or written that note."

"I'm not going to argue with you there."

"I was stupid." Ryder hung his head. "I let this depression spiral me down instead of turning to you. I'm sorry, baby."

"Don't be." Dean put his other hand on Ryder's hip and squeezed. "You had so much going on. I wish I could've been there but I'm here now and that's all that matters."

"I couldn't even look at it for the first week," Ryder confessed. "I haven't even actually admitted it out loud."

Dean moved so that he sat beside Ryder. "You can say it."

"My leg is gone... And it's not going to ever come back," Ryder said, voice catching.

Dean drew Ryder into an embrace and pressed a kiss to his hair. "I know, Ry. I'm so sorry."

"Please, don't ever look at me the way Ben did," Ryder whispered. "If you ever did... I'd... I can tell you're hiding something when you look it."

"I'm just sad that this happened, babe. That's all." Dean held him tighter. "Is he the reason you thought you wouldn't be attractive? Wait, is he even gay? Because I so didn't see that."

"Closeted big time." Ryder sighed. "Long story I'm too tired for, but yeah, he looks at me different now."

"Well, short story is he's an idiot." Dean got Ryder to

chuckle. He caressed Ryder's leg. "I meant every word at the hospital. You're beautiful to me. With one leg, no legs, or whatever." He turned Ryder's face and let him see the truth in his eyes. "This is the only way I'm ever going to look at you. Promise."

Ryder wrapped his arms around Dean and kissed him softly. He didn't say anything for a moment then, "How the hell did I get so lucky?"

"No, that's me." Dean put Ryder's hand over his heart. "You can't see my scars, Ry, but they're here. Something broke in me when I lost my brother, it hurt so bad and I was depressed too. Then we started writing our letters and you took away the hurt, the loneliness, and helped me through it all. I couldn't have done that without you."

"And I can't do this without you," Ryder said, pressing his hand to Dean's chest.

"I'm not going anywhere," Dean promised, sealing it with a kiss. "I'm right here, whatever you need."

Ryder's lips curled into a smile. "I just need you."

Chapter Seventeen

There was a tap at the doorframe, and Dean glanced up from grading papers to see his fellow teacher and best friend, Michael. Michael taught drama. He wore an outfit he'd probably made himself—patched blue jeans, a plain blue shirt and a jacket that resembled a chessboard—he had a flair for dramatics. His ash brown hair was artfully styled and he had jade green eyes. "Hey, Mike." Dean wrote B+ then capped his red felt pen. "How's it going?"

"Just wanted to see if we were still doing the writers' group at your place Friday."

"Crap, I forgot with everything going on. Um, let me run it by Ryder and I'll call you tonight."

Michael pulled the door closed. "So I take it things went well?"

"Yes and no." Dean stood and grabbed an eraser to clean the board before his next class. As he prepared, he filled Michael in. His friend sat on one of the desks, gaping.

"Wow, life really does suck sometimes." Michael gave him a sad look. "I'm so sorry about that. I can't even imagine what Ryder must be going through."

"I know, it's been so hard on him and I wish I could do more. I'm doing all I can, though, to make him see I'm not going anywhere."

"He's just scared," Michael said in understanding. "It's a hell of a commitment for anyone to make."

"He's worth it," Dean said without hesitation. "I had every intention of starting a relationship when he got home. I'm not letting this change that."

"Good for you. I'm sure it'll take time for you both to

adjust and figure things out. If you ever need to talk you know where my classroom is."

Dean grinned. "Thanks, Mike. That means a lot." He paused. "I'm kinda flying blind here. I just hope Ryder knows how much I care."

"Have you told him?"

"I want to. We… Well, it's almost been a week and we've been together every day."

"Have you…?"

"Mike!" Dean shook his head. "I don't kiss and tell."

"No, that's me." Michael winked. "And usually you live vicariously through me so c'mon, spill some details."

Dean chuckled. "Just his kisses get me going," he confessed, feeling his face heat up. "And we did have sex once. Not all the way but still… Damn, it was frakkin' incredible."

A grin split Michael's face. "Go on, I bet he's got a bod like Adonis."

"Oh he does." Dean tried not to think about it because here was the last place he needed to be having dirty thoughts. "I'm trying not to pressure him. I know he's working through issues. But damn, Mike, every night he lays with me I just want to…"

"Hump like bunnies?" Michael laughed and folded his hands together. "I say go for it, honey. You wanna work through his issues, show him how bad you want him."

"You think so?" Dean couldn't believe he was taking his friend's advice. Michael was a great guy, an even better friend, and funny. But he was also a big flirt who hopped from one guy's bed to the next. Though he could sure charm the pants off anyone.

"Yes, and if you need to get creative to help Ryder just call me because you know I've got plenty of tricks," Michael said, his eyes twinkling.

The bell rang as Dean chuckled. "I'll remember that."

* * * *

Curled up on the front porch swing, Ryder was lost in his sketches. Sassy had her head in his lap and Bones was at his feet. Feet—he smiled to himself as he realized he was starting to think of his prosthesis as his new leg. He had drawn all the surrounding homes then gone on to draw ideas of ways to expand their house. Then he'd had an even better idea of sketching the home he'd like to create for himself and Dean. He imagined a room with floor to ceiling bookshelves on the walls, all filled with books, and a reading area and desk for Dean's office and library. Oh sure, it was a little over the top, but it felt good dreaming again. Plus, it'd make Dean smile, and he loved seeing that.

He was so immersed that he didn't hear the gate open but he did look up as Bones ran off. Sassy, however, sat up, tail wagging but remaining by his side. A pretty redhead, two Starbucks coffees in hand, came up the porch. Sassy barked and the woman rolled her eyes.

"Seriously, Sassy?" She smiled at Ryder. "Hi, I'm Jessie."

Ryder put down his sketchpad and got to his feet. He returned the smile and held out a hand. She handed him a cup then shook it. "Ryder, but I'm guessing you know that."

"Yep." Jessie set her coffee on the little patio table then knelt down so she could hug Bones who was waiting patiently for attention. "Oh I miss you, buddy."

"He's a great dog." Ryder picked up Sassy. "And you, quit the barking or Dean will hear about it." Jessie laughed with Ryder as Sassy jumped down and ran off.

"Yeah, they both are. I can't wait to move into my apartment next month so I can bring Bones home."

Ryder took his seat again and Jessie joined him. "Thanks for the coffee."

"I may have texted and asked Dean what you like." Jessie brushed her hair back behind her ear. "I just wanted to come by and meet the guy who's got him smiling again."

Sipping his caramel macchiato, Ryder felt happiness bubble up at her words. "Well, I haven't had much to smile about lately but now he's been giving me reason to..."

Jessie put her hand on his knee, and surprise lit up her features as she likely felt the compression sock through his sweats. "Oh! I thought it was your other leg. I'm so sorry. I didn't hurt you, did I?" She flushed bright red.

Ryder squeezed her hand. "No, don't worry." He was a little shocked. "You really can't tell?"

She seemed genuinely honest. "No, you stood up and I couldn't even see a difference in your legs. Dean told me but if I hadn't known I wouldn't have guessed."

"I favor one leg when I walk but I don't know, I guess I was being paranoid thinking everyone would notice." Maybe it was like being gay—people didn't know until they got to know him, then if they cared they just accepted it. If they didn't then, oh well. Ryder realized he just needed to have that perspective. This was a part of who he was and it didn't matter what others thought. He just needed to be okay with it. And Dean was too, so why the worry?

"Unless you wear shorts I don't think anyone will." Jessie smiled. "Even if they do, it's no big deal. Well, it is a biggie how you saved another guy's life, that's what everyone will be talking about."

"Everyone acts like I was a hero. I just acted," Ryder told her. "I was terrified. I kept thinking how I'd never make it home." Jessie's eyes filled with tears and Ryder could've kicked himself. "Gosh, Jessie. I'm sorry."

"No, don't be. I just always wonder what Dax thought." She sniffled. "We never got the full story... I just hope he didn't suffer." She wiped at her eyes. "I'm glad you made it home, Ryder. I think it would've killed Dean if he lost you too."

Ryder nodded. "I know how hard this has been on him. And you, too."

Jessie wrapped her arms around Bones as he stood up and rested his paws on her thighs. It was like the dog sensed she needed comfort. She hugged Bones. "I just take it day by day. That's all we can ever really do."

"You're right. It'll get better with time." Ryder fell silent for a moment. He didn't know what else to say. There was no way to fix this, no way to heal the hurt. Dax was gone. Again, it hit him how lucky he was. He was here, in love with a good man, who needed him as much as he did. Together they'd get through all this. "I know I'm lucky, Jessie. I promise you I won't ever hurt Dean. He... I'm in love with him."

"When did you know?"

"It's going to sound crazy but there was this one time my CO was being a jerk, the day had gone to shit with a close call, and I was ready to lose it. I called Dean, just to hear his voice. He knew something was wrong—though I'm not sure how—and he said to me, just close your eyes. I did, and he sang this song to me, and everything else faded away and those five minutes were like a gift." Ryder broke into a grin. "And then we met. I stupidly tried pushing him away but the moment I saw him, I just knew there was no way I could let him go even if it was selfish."

"Selfish?"

"This is a lot to ask of him."

"No, it's not. You're not asking, he wants to be with you. He wants what you do." Jessie turned to him. "I've never seen Dean care about anyone the way he does with you. He's always been so guarded."

"Because of his bio parents."

"They were supposed to love him unconditionally, I can't even understand how they could do that to their own child," Jessie said sadly. "But I know how much it hurt him. When Dax died I saw those walls go right back up—he was ready to close himself off again, I could see it. And then to my surprise he didn't. Because of you."

"We have that in common. My mom gave me up, and my love life before this was disastrous. I don't trust easy or let my guard down but Dean just slipped right in," Ryder told her.

"Have you told him you love him?"

"Not yet. I want it to be the right moment, cheesy as that sounds."

"That's sweet." Jessie squeezed his hand. "I like you, Ryder. I know you and Dean are going to be okay. This will all work out, trust me."

"You know I do believe that." Ryder put his coffee down. "I'd like us to be friends. I've got therapy but how about lunch afterwards?"

"Sounds good to me. You need a ride?"

Ryder gave her a quick hug. He could see the two of them becoming good friends. "I was going to call Beth but if you don't mind? I've gotta learn to drive again."

"No trouble at all."

91

Chapter Eighteen

"Are you sure you don't want to go to a movie or something?" Dean asked, setting out the chips and dip. He was nervous about Ryder meeting his friends. Oh, he knew his friends would like Ryder but he was afraid of how boring this would all seem to him.

Ryder leaned against the wall. "You don't want me to meet your friends?" He sounded a little hurt.

"No! I just… They're writers, teachers, geeks… And I love every one of them and to us this is fun. But I don't want to bore you. I don't want… Never mind."

"No, what?"

"I worry that with the exciting life you've led this will all be dull to you and you won't like it," Dean admitted quietly.

Ryder made his way to him. "I'm done living life in the fast lane. Not just because of my leg but because I want this." He gestured out. "A quiet night in with your friends. No danger, no fear, nothing to worry about." He took Dean's hand. "This isn't boring, this is what I want. You're sharing your interests with me and when I'm a little stronger I'll share some of mine."

"I like to hike," Dean agreed.

"See? And maybe we could go to the gun range and I could teach you to shoot at targets."

"No hunting, though?" Dean didn't want to kill anything. Though it could be fun to have Ryder show him how to handle a gun. Not that he didn't know how, thanks to Dax, but a few brush-up lessons might be needed. That thought reminded him of how sexy his lover was in his fatigues and sparked a few ideas.

"No. And we both like cooking. And watching *Game of Thrones*." Ryder twined their fingers together. "I promise you I'm not bored. And I'm not going to be." He kissed Dean's temple. "How could I be when I have you?"

Dean broke into a smile. He leaned in and kissed Ryder softly, showing him what those words meant to him. Sometimes this felt like an amazing dream and he was scared he'd wake up and be all alone. Then Ryder would say just the right thing and the worry would disappear. "My friends are excited to meet you. Michael's a little over the top, but you'll get used to it."

Ryder chuckled. "Am I going to get the third degree as the new boyfriend?"

"Probably." Dean chewed on his bottom lip. "They know I've never lived with another guy before so they probably will have questions."

Ryder seemed surprised. "You haven't?"

Dean wasn't sure he could explain it, but he'd try. If anyone could understand it'd be Ryder. He'd said as much before. "I never wanted to risk losing my home again. I saved up to rent this place. Now I've got a mortgage, and it is mine. No one can kick me out or take away everything…"

Ryder drew him into an embrace. "I didn't realize how big of a deal it was to let me stay, baby. Thank you. It means a lot that you trust me. I hope you know I'd never do that."

"I do. Up until you came along no one else was worth the risk. Now, it's not just a place I want to call mine. I want it to be ours." Dean wrapped his arms around Ryder. He was starting to feel like wherever Ryder was, that was home.

"So do I." Ryder's lips quirked into a smile. Dean wanted to kiss him again but the doorbell rang.

"That'll be Michael. He's always early." After scooping up Sassy, he took Ryder's hand and they went to answer the door.

Michael, holding a plate full of finger foods, gave them a big grin. "Well, hello, gorgeous. Now I see why Dean has been walking around with a huge smile."

Dean shook his head, trying not to blush. "Ryder, meet Michael. Michael, behave yourself."

"As if." Michael stepped in and kissed Ryder's cheek. "Nice to meet you."

"Likewise." Ryder held out a hand. "Can I take this for you?"

"And a gentleman to boot." Michael whistled. "Damn, Dean, you'd better claim him before I do."

Ryder laughed as Dean felt himself flush red. Ryder took the plate. "Oh he has, don't worry about that."

"Ooh, details!" Michael followed Ryder to the kitchen. Slapping a hand to his face, Dean just went along, wondering why he had thought this was a good idea.

After he set the plate on the counter, Ryder turned to Michael. "I don't kiss and tell."

With a pout, Michael replied, "Dean said that then I wormed details out of him." He shrugged. "What can I say? I've hit a dry spell, just looking for a little excitement."

"Well, go to the bar," Dean teased, leaning against the counter. "Because I'm not sharing."

"Or I'll become a pen pal and get my own sexy soldier." Michael winked at Ryder. "So, who else is coming tonight?"

Dean set Sassy down as she was getting antsy in his arms. She barked at Michael then ran off. "Bryan and Jules, you know they're never on time."

"Everything set up?" When Dean nodded, Michael added, "You have any stories for us, Ryder?"

"'Fraid not, I'm not a writer. Though I do draw."

"Oh, can I see?" Michael held out his hands in a pleading gesture. "You never know, one day one of us might need an illustrator."

"I'm not sure I'm that good," Ryder replied. "I am going to try and get a degree in architecture this fall."

"Good for you. Where at?"

"Fayetteville."

Dean listened as he set out the finger food Michael had

brought, happy that Ryder and his best friend were getting along. *One down, two to go.* Though he didn't doubt Ryder could win them over too. He just had a way about him—everyone loved him as soon as they met him. *Though not as much as me.*

****

Listening to everyone's stories was actually interesting, Ryder thought. And some of the scenes Michael had read aloud were hotter than hell. Damn, there was no way this could be considered dull. He chimed in with his own ideas and found himself having a good time. He liked how the critique was both honest and helpful. It was clear that all three men were encouragement to one another and that they loved to write. Ryder believed they were all good enough to be published—especially Dean with his dragon shifter story. He was hoping to bribe Dean with some kissing and maybe more later to read the next chapter.

After the readings, they all sat around, laughing, chatting and having a good time. Bryan was as big a fan as Ryder was of baseball and the Braves so they started talking stats. Dean went to get more sodas and Ryder watched Jules follow after. The platinum blond in skinny jeans clearly had a crush on Dean, though Ryder wasn't so sure Dean had even noticed. Still, he wondered what was going on so he told Bryan he'd be right back and made his way to the kitchen.

Neither Dean nor Jules noticed him so he hung back, watching Dean grab a bottle of Pepsi from the fridge. "So, what did you wanna talk about, Jul?"

"You and Ryder are serious?"

Dean gave Jules a 'well duh' look and Ryder almost chuckled. "You knew that already. I told you guys before I had every intention of this being serious when he got home."

"But—"

"If you say anything about his leg, I might hit you," Dean warned and Ryder's heart skipped. "I don't give a damn about that."

"No, not that," Jules said in a rush. "Are you sure you know Ryder that well to have him living here?"

Dean pulled some plastic cups out of their packaging. "Here I thought you'd be happy for me," he said, "not questioning my choices."

"I'm sorry," Jules said. "It's just fast, you gotta admit that. You've always been the one who takes time with things but ever since Ryder came along you've changed."

Pouring the soda, Dean glared at his friend. "So? It's not okay now for me to be happy and just enjoy life? I thought after all I've been through I deserve a little happiness."

"I'm not saying that." Jules sighed. "It's just you met him and then three days later he's moved in."

"We've talked for a year. I know Ry." Dean poked Jules in the chest. "What is your problem, huh?"

"My problem is why couldn't it have been me?" Jules blurted out, then his eyes widened and he nearly slapped his hand over his mouth.

Gaping at him, Dean clearly couldn't believe what he'd just heard, confirming Ryder's earlier thoughts. "What?"

"We've been friends since middle school and you've never noticed me," Jules said sadly. "All I've ever been is your friend, even after that one time in high school when we kissed—"

"We were drunk, it shouldn't have happened," Dean apologized. "If I had known you liked me I'd have never—"

"Well you did," Jules interrupted, then hastily added, "but it was my fault too. I wanted to tell you so many times but I was scared that you'd reject me. So, I kept waiting, hoping that maybe one day you'd see me, but then Ryder shows up and now I'm never going to get my chance to show you how I feel…"

"I'm sorry, Jul," Dean said quietly. "I don't know what you want me to say, I can't help who I fall for or don't."

"Why him and not me?" Jules repeated, hurt lacing his tone.

"I'm not going to compare you two. That's not fair," Dean argued, "All I'll say is the day Ryder wrote me, I just knew he came into my life for a reason. I care about him, I have feelings for him, and I'm sure as hell not going to give him up just because my friends think I'm moving too fast. My choice is him."

"What if I told you I loved you?" Jules stepped closer, trapping Dean against the counter. Ryder bit back a growl, but didn't move.

"I don't have feelings for you," Dean said and Ryder knew it was the truth. "I don't see you that way, I'm sorry."

"Are you sure?" Jules pleaded, putting his hand over Dean's as he tried to push him away.

Before Ryder could step in, Jules grabbed Dean in desperation and tried kissing him. After shoving him away, Dean put some distance between them, thankfully stopping it from happening. "What the fuck? How dare you!"

"I'm sorry," Jules said hurriedly. "I just wanted to kiss you so badly and I'd give anything to change your mind."

Ryder wanted to barge in and knock the guy into next week, but Dean was doing a good job all on his own with letting Jules have it. "Well it won't change," Dean said angrily. "You had no right. What am I going to do now, huh? I'll have to tell Ry and how can you be here for the writers' group if I can't trust you?"

"I was just overwhelmed and didn't think. I swear it'll never happen again." Jules's look was pleading. "I get it, okay? We'll just pretend this never happened. You don't have to tell Ryder."

That was enough for Ryder. He revealed himself and Jules jumped. "Tell me what?"

Dean spun around. "Ry, did you hear all that?"

Face pale and clearly terrified, Jules ran from the room. Moments later they heard the front door open then shut.

"Sure did." Ryder leaned against the fridge. "I saw during

the session he was crushing on you. When I saw him follow you, I got curious."

Running a hand back through his hair, Dean said, "I had no idea. All this time and he's never said a word then it all comes out and I feel terrible for not noticing."

"It's not your fault," Ryder reasoned, "If he wanted you to know he should've said something before."

Dean moved over to him and looked him in the eye. "I told him, Ry, *you* are my choice."

With a soft smile, Ryder tugged Dean into his arms. He brushed their lips together. "I heard, baby. And I trust you."

"But I don't trust him now... I don't want to lose him as a friend but nothing is going to be the same," Dean said sadly. "How can it be?"

"I'm sorry." Ryder cupped Dean's cheek and gazed at him. "I may be angry at him for almost kissing you—you're mine." He pressed a kiss to Dean's lips possessively. "But I understand he's your friend and I get why he has feelings for you. And I'll support whatever choice you make. Just know I'm right here, okay?"

"Have I told you today how amazing you are?" Dean smiled at him. "How happy you make me?"

"As happy as you made me hearing I was your choice," Ryder breathed against Dean's lips.

Dean pressed him against the fridge, the coolness a stark contrast to Dean's warm body, it felt damn good. He pulled Dean in for another kiss, losing himself in it, as his hands roamed over his lover's body.

Michael wolf-whistled as he walked past and picked up a cup of soda. "Sorry, thirsty. Please don't stop on my account. Though, PS, what sent Julesy running?"

They broke apart, Dean turning toward Michael and Ryder wrapping his arms around him from behind. "He tried to tell me he loved me and almost kissed me."

Holding up a hand, Michael's eyes widened. "No, he didn't. I'm going to talk to him. I told him before he needs to get over that crush and not spoil things. Damn that boy."

"Wait, you knew?"

Michael shrugged. "I figured it out this year, and Jules confirmed it after he told me but I think everyone but you knew."

"Why didn't you tell me?" Dean asked, clearly frustrated. Ryder rubbed his hip, trying to soothe him.

"Because Dax died and you were broken. Seriously. Jules could never be what you need, but Ryder is and I know that even more now," Michael admitted, turning serious as he gave them both a look. "Jules does too, that's why he went off the rails tonight, but he'll accept it and be back to apologize, you'll see."

Dean sighed. He leaned back into Ryder, reaching for his hand. "He'll have to accept it. Otherwise he can stay the hell away from me."

"Baby." Ryder kissed his shoulder.

"No. I'm really happy. Story of my life is that usually gets taken away somehow. I'm not letting anything make that happen."

"It won't. Not gonna happen, not this time," Ryder promised.

* * * *

Later that night when they were lying in bed, Ryder picked up where he and Dean had left off when Michael had interrupted them. He worshiped Dean's body, from head to toe. He caressed and kissed every inch of his lover. He already knew where Dean was most sensitive, that a nip to his ear would cause him to make a sexy growl in the back of his throat. A moan escaped with the caress of his hipbone. He gasped when Ryder licked his inner thigh. And Dean began to mutter and plead when he kissed the head of his cock.

He blew Dean, and even teased his entrance a bit. He wanted to go further, open him up and claim Dean as his, make love to him. But he didn't. He couldn't. He was more confident now, yet still had his doubts. He knew he could satisfy Dean this way, but would he be able to take him? How would he keep his balance? Rhythm? He worried it'd be a disaster that would leave Dean disappointed. That scared him. Things were going so well and he didn't want to mess it up.

So he denied himself the pleasure, using his hand to jack off as he sucked Dean until he cried out and came deep in his throat. He orgasmed with his lover. Dean released the tight grip on his hair and pulled him up for a kiss, chasing his taste from Ryder's mouth. It was sweet and unhurried, both of them sated.

"What about you?" Dean drew one of his legs up, seeming to hint at offering himself up.

"I came just from that," Ryder told him with a smile. "You were so damn sexy I couldn't help it."

"Well, how about—?" Dean's look was tender as Ryder stifled a yawn. He hoped Dean would suggest they get some sleep. He knew Dean wanted more too, and eventually they'd have to talk, but not tonight.

"I'm sorry, guess I'm tired." Ryder spooned into Dean's side.

"Yeah, it's late." Dean kissed his temple and held onto him. "I've gotta be up early."

"How about I make omelets in the morning?" They were Dean's favorite.

"Mm, you're spoiling me." Dean grinned. "Only if I get to return the favor in the morning."

"Deal." Ryder closed his eyes and feigned drifting off to sleep with Dean. What if he wasn't enough? Dean's words from earlier rang in his head. His lover was happy. Ryder simply had to build up the courage and take the next step toward being more intimate. He wasn't going to lose him over this, he had to figure out a way around his limitation then he could make love to Dean. He'd just have to get a little more creative.

Chapter Nineteen

It'd been a month. An amazing month, but a month nonetheless. He and Ryder had grown closer every day, they'd started building a life together and had a routine. Intimately, it hadn't gone further than hand jobs and blow jobs. Dean wanted more. He craved it, but it seemed as if Ryder was scared to go that far. Oh sure, Dean knew they'd have to get a little creative but he was willing to do almost anything to have Ryder make love to him. So he decided to take matters into his own hands tonight.

He had slowly and methodically removed every bit of Ryder's clothing, kissing and caressing every inch of skin as it had been revealed. Ryder had practically torn off his clothes then they had undulated against each other, kissing and letting the pleasure slowly coil up until he had begged for more. Which was where they were now — Ryder's fingers tangled in Dean's hair as he nibbled and sucked on his lover's neck, a vivid love bite appearing.

"Dean," Ryder moaned as Dean moved his hands to his chest.

He couldn't resist gently pinching one of Ryder's dusky nipples. Ryder arched up into it.

Dean smirked as he looked up. "Like that, huh?" He kissed Ryder then grabbed his lover's hands and moved them up above his head where he held them in place. "I don't want you to move," he ordered. "Let me do all the work. I have plans and you're going to love them, but I want you to do as I say. Can you?"

Ryder met his gaze, eyes darkening with arousal. He clearly liked Dean taking control — so far so good. "Oh fuck, you're being sexy as hell right now," Ryder breathed. "Yeah, I'll do whatever you say, baby."

"Good. Now just enjoy." Dean brushed their lips together.

Ryder seemed to be trying his best not to move, though Dean felt the tremor run through his lover as he ran a hand over his taut stomach. He bent his head and sucked and teased Ryder's erect nipple. He soothed it gently with his tongue before moving on to the other and doing the same until Ryder was crying out and clutching the pillow under his head with both of his fists.

"Want me to keep going?" Dean teased, loving how he was driving Ryder crazy with just his touch.

"Yeah, don't stop. Please."

Dean kissed along Ryder's stomach, mapping his lover's body with his mouth, tongue and teeth mostly to tease but also because he loved the taste of Ryder's skin. Ryder was panting and making small sounds of pleasure that brought a smile to Dean's face. He licked Ryder's navel, causing him to arch up.

Pausing for a moment, Dean couldn't help but stare. Ryder looked utterly wanton and stunning with his flawless skin, toned muscles, firm chest and lovely cock. A surge of possessives rose up and he wanted to claim his lover. He left a love bite on Ryder's hip, then continued exploring Ryder's body. He pressed kisses to Ryder's inner thighs, his hips, his balls and entrance. He drew one of Ryder's balls into his mouth then the other, avoiding his lover's straining erection. He added into the mix, pressing his fingers against Ryder's hips, keeping him in place.

"God, Dean!" Ryder cried out, writhing under him. "You're driving me crazy!"

Dean grinned. "Am I?" He ran his hand across Ryder's thigh. He wanted Ryder lost in desire, so desperate he wouldn't say no to what he had planned. He knew Ryder wanted him — he just needed to see how bad Dean needed him too. He planted a trail of kisses down Ryder's cock, before taking the head in his mouth and licking the slit, savoring Ryder's essence.

Ryder gasped as Dean encircled the crown. Dean rubbed his tongue along the underside of the head and Ryder moaned, clutching tightly onto the pillow. Dean swallowed Ryder whole, deep-throating his lover easily as he felt himself harden in response. He began slowly sliding up and down Ryder's shaft, taking him deep then sucking hard until he reached the very tip, over and over until Ryder was bucking into his mouth. Ryder was crying out Dean's name, ready to fall over the edge, and Dean knew he was too close. He pulled away and up, not wanting Ryder to come. He knew what he wanted—Ryder buried deep inside him as they made love.

He crawled up Ryder's body, capturing his lips in a hungry kiss as Ryder moaned desperately, tasting himself on his Dean's tongue. "Shh, if you had come we couldn't do what I want," he breathed against Ryder's lips. He pressed his ass against Ryder's dick. "Just hang on for me, babe. I promise it'll be worth it."

Ryder whimpered but then the haze of arousal faded in his eyes a little. He moved his hands and clutched Dean's arms. "Wait…"

"Ry," Dean said, trying to hide his frustration. "I need you so much. I can't stop thinking about this. Please, babe, tell me why. Why, when I want you to make love to me?"

Reaching up, Ryder cupped his face. "I'm not sure I can give you what you need. You say all we have to do is get a little creative but what if it's no good for you? What if I can't pleasure you?"

"You can and you will," Dean said confidently, gazing down at Ryder. "Because it's not just physical, Ry. Even though I'm dying right now, it's about our connection. I want you in me, please. Trust me, and just go with what feels good. I know I'm going to be satisfied and so will you."

Ryder drew him down for a tender kiss that told Dean how much Ryder loved him even if he hadn't said the words yet. He couldn't now. He didn't want Ryder thinking he had said it because of the heat of the moment. "Okay, baby. I trust you." Ryder whimpered and leaned up for another kiss. "You're going to ride me?"

"Yep, I am." Dean grinned as he reached over and into the nightstand for the lube. "I'm going to show you how easy this is going to be for us." He saw the condoms, but he'd gotten tested before Ryder had come home and Ryder had gotten a clean bill of health at the hospital. "Do you want a rubber?"

"No, I want to feel you." Ryder brushed his leg. "I'm sorry for putting the brakes on. I just don't want to disappoint you." He smiled softly. "I can't stop thinking about this either, though, every night lying here with you…"

Dean kissed him again. "No more denying what we both want, yeah?"

"Yeah. I need you."

"Watch me then."

Ryder growled. "You're going to kill me."

"But what a way to go," Dean retorted and Ryder laughed.

"Oh hell yeah, the very best way."

Dean chuckled as he straddled Ryder thighs, his erection rubbing against Ryder's, causing both of them to moan. Dean popped open the lid and lubed up his fingers then reached behind himself, sliding one in and groaning as he worked it slowly inside his body. Locking his eyes with his lover, Dean inserted a second and began to rock backwards, impaling himself then thrusting forward to rub his cock against Ryder's.

Ryder bit his lip. Dean could see his lover's arousal had returned and he was fighting the urge to remain still. To his surprise, Ryder asked, "What are you thinking about?"

"You. I'm thinking of your fingers inside me. How I love you doing this. Feels amazing." Dean added a third finger and moaned softly, all thoughts fleeing as he focused on Ryder and the love he felt from his lover.

"I want to be inside you, Dean," Ryder said huskily. "I want you to ride me."

"Yes!" Dean threw his head back in pleasure. "I need you, Ry."

Ryder put his hands on Dean's hips, then he reached for the lube and handed it to Dean. Dean removed his fingers from his entrance then intertwining his hand with Ryder's they slicked Ryder's shaft with lube. He rose up and moved forward so that his opening was positioned over Ryder's cock. The broad head of Ryder's cock had a drop of pre-cum.

"Ready?" Dean asked.

"Shouldn't I ask you that?" Ryder joked.

"Touché."

Not wanting to wait a second more, Dean plunged downward, crying out as he impaled himself fully on Ryder in one swift movement. He threw his head back again. It burned as he was stretched but was so damn good. "Oh God, yes!" It was better than he'd ever imagined—Ryder fit inside him perfectly. He had never been so full and he had no idea he could feel so good.

"Just like that!" Ryder cried, pulling Dean down for a messy kiss as their bodies adjusted to each other. "You okay, baby?" He brushed the sweaty hair off Dean's forehead.

"Hell yeah. You feel amazing," Dean mumbled against Ryder's lips.

"So do you," Ryder whispered, nudging Dean back upright. "Go ahead, baby. Ride me hard."

Dean reached for his lover's hands. Intertwining their fingers, he began to move, using the combined strength of their arms for leverage. He quickly found a perfect rhythm, one that Ryder could meet with thrusts of his own. Ryder braced his foot on the bed so he could thrust harder and deeper as he urged Dean on. Passion took over at that point and Dean lost himself in how complete he felt with Ryder in him and holding him.

Slowly at first than faster, Dean impaled himself repeatedly on Ryder's shaft, angling his descent each time so that Ryder struck his prostate over and over. He rode

Ryder with a reckless abandon, moving up and down for some time with no thoughts but to give them both pleasure and chase his release. He tried to hold off as long as he could but it was all too much.

"So close, Ry," Dean panted. "Need to come."

Ryder moved their intertwined hands to Dean's cock and with swift, sure strokes drove Dean to the edge. "Come for me," he said. "I want to see you lose control — to know it's my body doing that to you."

"Yes! God! Yes!" Dean began to move faster. He guided Ryder's other hand with his own to his hip. The added pressure let him fuck himself even harder. "Ryder!" His orgasm hit him suddenly, nearly blinding him as he cried out and released streams of cum across his lover's chest and belly. He'd never come so hard before and nearly fell forward.

Ryder clenched Dean's waist tightly for a moment. He was still hard inside Dean. Dean gasped as Ryder pulled him down for a kiss. "Help me?" Ryder whispered then rolled them so that he was on top of Dean. He got himself up on his good knee and put his weight on his powerful forearms, which he braced on either side of Dean's head. Dean wrapped one leg around Ryder's waist, not wanting to let go. He braced his other leg against Ryder's side, supporting him so he didn't slip. Ryder's eyes filled with love and they kissed again. Dean tangled his fingers in Ryder's hair as Ryder broke the kiss and nipped his shoulder.

"See? Nothing to it." Dean smiled. "Let go, Ry. Make me yours."

"All mine." Ryder nipped harder then he whispered something that Dean couldn't make out.

Ryder pounded into Dean mercilessly as he worked toward his own release. Balls deep in him, Ryder's thrusts hit Dean's sensitized prostate in short, sharp jabs that had his spent dick twitching and gaining interest once more. He writhed and cried out. He'd thought it couldn't get any better but now, with Ryder taking control and claiming him so thoroughly, he was carried away on waves of pleasure. He might have even blacked out for a second.

Suddenly Ryder tensed. He tossed his head back and his shaft filled even further, then pulsed into Dean's willing, receptive body filling him in long, hard pulses that seemed to go on forever. Ryder cried out his name, shuddered then collapsed onto Dean's chest, his softening cock still inside him.

For long moments, they lay together, covered in sweat and cum with their chests heaving. Slowly, Ryder slid out, though Dean wanted him to stay. Still, he knew they had to clean up if they didn't want to get stuck together. He grabbed his discarded shirt and wiped them both off.

As Ryder watched Dean toss the shirt aside he knew he shouldn't have waited so long to finally make love to Dean. But it had been worth it. Their connection, their love for one another and the sex itself—Ryder knew it didn't get any better than this. Still, he had to quell his insecurity and quietly asked, "So, not to stroke my own ego but, um, was it good, baby?"

Dean chuckled. "You have to ask? I came harder than I ever have. What does that tell you?"

"Well, you were so gorgeous riding me and, damn, you felt incredible. I already want you again." Ryder squeezed his ass and Dean moaned. "You up for it?"

Dean rubbed against him. "Not to stoke your ego, but after that we can go all night."

"Fuck yeah." Ryder held Dean closer. "I'm not going to be able to get enough of you now. I may never let you leave this bed."

"Is that so?"

"Hmm." Ryder brushed their lips together. "You're all mine now."

Dean kissed him long and slow, sending Ryder flying. "Yep, let me show you again."

* * * *

so thoroughly he was certain it was of pleasure.
He might, however, choked out for a second.

Afterward they lay tangled together, Dean's head pillowed on Ryder's chest, Ryder's hand idly rubbing his back. "We should have a barbecue before summer is over. We could invite some friends, make a party of it."

"That'd be fun. Joel would come."

"Bentley?"

Dean felt Ryder flinch. "I'd rather not invite him."

"I thought you were friends?"

"We pretend to be, mostly." Ryder sighed. "I do owe him for saving my life but still... It'd be awkward since I've avoided talking to him lately."

Dean didn't like where this was going. His stomach twisted in knots. "Is there something I should know?"

"Yeah... I suppose I should just start from the beginning." Ryder cleared his throat. "I met Ben when I was seventeen. I ran away from the group home and he was another kid on the streets. He stopped some asshats from beating me up. I ended up crushing on him. We both got jobs, rented a crappy place and tried to figure out a way to get out of our shitty lives. We were fooling around but it wasn't serious to him. Our solution was joining the Army. We thought we'd see the world together. I felt like it would give me a purpose, let me make a difference. Ben just wanted power and prestige... Anyway, we passed boot camp. Before our first tour Ben gave me an ultimatum. Break it off or keep it secret — you know, don't ask, don't tell..."

"That son of a bitch," Dean said angrily.

"Yeah, I thought so too. But I was a stupid kid just turned eighteen. I was scared of being alone. I gave in for a while. I thought I could change his mind, that maybe he'd come out for us. When he told me about finding a girlfriend I was crushed, broke it off and cut all ties with him outside the Army. He tried for a few years to get back with me — he wanted a guy on the side — but I'm no one's doormat, damn it."

"Hell no, you're not." Dean moved so they were face to face. "Damn, Ry. I'm sorry he did that to you."

"Me too. Really messed me up," he admitted, voice catching. "All my life, Dean, everyone has run away from me. My mother dropped me off at a firehouse and didn't look back. My foster homes would take me in only to bring me right back. Ben ran from who I was... I just don't get it. What is it about me that makes everyone leave?"

Dean cupped his cheek. His heart broke at the pain in Ryder's eyes. He had to comfort him, take it away. "I'm not going anywhere. You believe that, don't you?"

Ryder locked gazes with him. "Yeah, I do. For the first time in my life, I really do."

Dean still saw the insecurity and understood. His parents had tossed him aside, his college lover had moved to the other side of the country, Dax had joined the Army then he'd lost him. He'd had those same thoughts and said as much to Ryder.

Gently Dean bumped his knee against Ryder's injured one. "I'm not running away from this because there's no reason to. I'm not leaving you," he repeated. "And I'll tell you why. Because I love you, Ryder." He moved so he was lying over Ryder and cradled his face. "There's nothing that could make me love you less."

A tear slid down Ryder's cheek and Dean thumbed it away. "I love you, too. So much," he whispered, lifting his head to kiss Dean softly. "He might have stopped me from dying, but you've kept me alive. You don't ever have to worry because I'm yours. Just yours."

Dean broke into a smile and covered Ryder in kisses. He knew that, he could feel it. He was happy and loved. It was incredible and terrifying all at once. He was vulnerable but he knew Ryder wouldn't hurt him, not like everyone else had. He could trust his heart with Ryder. And he did. "And I'm yours."

Chapter Twenty

It was a warm, sunny day with a cool breeze — perfect weather for a outdoor party. Dean invited his friends, Ryder invited Joel and a few of the guys he knew still on base. Bentley showed up with Joel, who had let it slip unknowingly since he didn't know they didn't want Bentley to come. Ryder hoped he wouldn't cause any trouble. On top of that, after not seeing him for a month, Jules dropped by as well, but he apologized and he and Dean talked, though Ryder had to hold himself back when he saw them hug. His damn insecurity had him wondering for a moment if he could be enough, but then Dean turned his smile on him, kissed him in front of everyone, and proudly told them that Ryder would be receiving a medal for his bravery — from the President, no less, for gallantry above and beyond the call of duty. He couldn't believe it. He was a bit embarrassed over all the attention, but touched when everyone cheered.

Joel helped him man the barbecue. "I see Ben is being awfully quiet."

Adding a few burgers to the grill, Ryder replied, "Hopefully not the calm before the storm."

With a glance back, Joel's eyes widened. "I think I missed something."

Nodding, Ryder filled Joel in with a brief explanation then added, "I don't think he'll do anything, but he's got a short fuse."

"I'm sorry, if I'd known I'd have kept my big mouth shut."

"Don't worry about it." Ryder clapped his shoulder. "So, you want to add the seasonings? You gotta tell me your secrets on how you get these burgers to taste so good."

"If I told you I'd have to kill you," Joel joked and they both laughed.

Ryder was roasting hot dogs when Jules came over. "Um, can I please talk to you? Just for a sec."

He wiped his hands on a dishtowel, then passed the tongs to Joel. "Be right back."

He followed Jules to the side of the house as the younger man twisted his hands. "I just wanted to say sorry, Ryder. I hope you're not angry with me. I, uh, I miss Dean like crazy. His friendship means a lot to me and I know if I don't fix things that I'll lose it."

"Funny way of showing that," Ryder couldn't help but say.

"Huh?"

"Look, I get why you love him, Jules. How could you not? I've known him a year and I can't imagine life without him," Ryder admitted. "You grew up with him, I really do get it. What angers me is you hurt him. You made him think your friendship is one big lie and that the only reason you've stayed around is for the chance to be with him. And after everything he's gone through that's just wrong."

"It's not like that at all," Jules argued. "His friendship means everything to me."

"Yet you disrespected him and kept yourself hidden," Ryder pointed out with a sad shake of his head. "You took it a step further and disrespected our relationship by trying to kiss him."

"I am sorry about that," Jules said, hanging his head. "Really."

"I know Dean forgave you, it's who he is. He wants you in his life and I respect that. It's his choice." Ryder took a step closer, crowding Jules, and his voice dropped dangerously low. "But I'm going to say this just once so listen carefully — you try anything like that again and you won't see me coming. Understood?"

With a gulp, Jules gave a shaky nod. "Understood."

"Good." Ryder managed a tight smile. "Then we can move on." He held out his hand and Jules warily accepted the gesture, relaxing a little when Ryder just shook it. "I love him, Jules. You don't have to worry about him being hurt. That's the last thing I'd ever do."

"Good, he deserves to be happy. I want him to be. And I'll support you guys from now on, promise." Jules gave Ryder a sad smile then hurried away.

"You threatening Jules?" Dean asked, slightly teasing and making Ryder almost jump.

He held up a tiny space between thumb and forefinger. "Just a bit, I hope you're not angry I did."

"I probably would be if I didn't know you were a big softie," Dean replied. "And you did it because you worry. I saw that look on your face earlier."

Ryder shrugged. "I can't help it sometimes, baby." He rubbed his bad leg. "I don't doubt your love. I've just got hang-ups that I'm getting over, thanks to you."

Dean cupped his face and brushed a featherlight kiss over his lips. "I know, and that's why it's taking all I got not to go kick Bentley's ass outta here."

"I don't get why he showed."

"Me either, you'd think he'd get the hint."

Ryder chuckled. "You'd think so, but then Ben was always an idiot at taking hints."

Hearing a call from Joel, Ryder stole a kiss then headed back out to help. A little while later, the party in full swing, he was a little tired of all the standing, so he used the excuse of taking a leak to go sit in the bedroom for a few. Sassy curled up with him, keeping him company.

When he felt better, Ryder stepped out of the bedroom and to his surprise found Bentley leaning against the hall wall. It almost felt as if he was cornering Ryder, though he didn't know why. His worry was confirmed when he tried to walk past and Bentley stepped in front of him.

"You've been avoiding me," Bentley accused.

"I've been busy making burgers," Ryder countered. "And

I need to get back to it, so would you mind?"

"Why didn't you invite me?" Bentley sounded almost hurt. "You've been avoiding me, we hardly talk anymore."

"You told me you were going on vacation with Rachel," Ryder lied. "I figured you'd be gone."

"No, you thought this would be awkward. Have you told Dean about us?"

"First, there is no us." Ryder glared. "Second, I guess I was right since you're making this awkward."

"I just want to talk," Bentley pleaded, "I miss you."

"I don't."

Ryder knew Bentley just wanted attention. He thought about pushing him aside but the fear of tripping stopped him. He took a step back as Bentley edged forward. He heard a growl and Sassy started pawing at the door.

"You're out of the Army now, we could have something. I saved your life, and now I want more of how it used to be. You remember how good it was? I do."

That shocked Ryder. He gaped. "Wait, what?"

"We'd still have to keep it secret, of course, but we could have fun like we used to." Bentley's hands framed his hips. "It could all work out. I'm sick of Rachel, I'm miserable." His eyes locked on Ryder's. "I never felt that way with you."

Ryder pointed at him. "I'm never going to be your goddamned dirty secret, Bentley. Ever! You made me miserable. You screwed me up so bad I could've blown things with Dean. So, no. Now please move."

Bentley didn't. Instead he moved closer, leaning in as if he intended to kiss Ryder. *Like hell he will.* He shoved his hands out, stopping Bentley and turning his face away.

Anger filled Bentley's features. He lashed out. "You're not a prize like this, Ryder. He'll get bored of you soon enough so don't come crying to me when he does, because I won't offer this again."

"Fuck you." Ryder pushed past Bentley.

Bentley grabbed his shoulder, swinging him around. The

momentum twisted his knee wrong and he stumbled in pain, falling.

Strong, loving arms caught him somehow. "Babe, are you okay?" Dean's voice was filled with concern.

Ryder held onto Dean tightly as he tried to get his balance. His leg hurt but he didn't think it was serious. "Think so," he murmured.

"Can you lean against the wall for a sec?" Dean asked and Ryder nodded, though he wasn't sure why Dean wanted him to do that.

Dean helped him move and he took a deep breath. He saw Bentley looking for an escape but before he could Dean grabbed him and struck out with his fist, connecting to Bentley's jaw. "You son of a bitch!" Dean yelled. "You could've set his recovery back by months. How dare you come into our home and make a pass at my partner and then hurt him."

Bentley rubbed his jaw, his other hand clenched. "He's tougher than that. Or do you not know him at all?"

With a roll of his eyes, Dean retorted, "I do, better than you ever have. And I heard what you just said. Ryder is amazing. Funny, sweet, strong, and a million other things. I will not let you hurt him again! He deserves the best. Not to be treated like that. I'd never force him to keep quiet to protect a stupid image." He glanced back at Ryder. "I'd shout it out to the whole world that he's mine." He pointed at Bentley. "You're the idiot who let him go. Just because he's happy now you don't get to make him miserable again so get the hell out of here before I make you."

"Hah," Bentley scoffed. "You think you can?"

"I think he can and I certainly will," Joel interjected, nearly making Ryder jump as he didn't notice he'd come inside. "You know how much I hate disrespect."

"Fine." Bentley shoved past them all and stormed to the front hall. "Your loss, Ryder." He turned back. "Watch pretty boy's back. This isn't over."

Ryder made to lunge forward but Dean held him back.

"You come near us again, Ben, and you'll regret it!"

Bentley slammed the door as he left and Ryder sagged back in Dean's arms. "Joel, I'm going to take Ry to rest for a minute, can you go tell everyone that everything is fine and distract them?"

"You got it."

"Joel," Ryder called out as he turned away. "Thanks, man."

"Anytime, Ryder." Joel winked and dashed through the kitchen.

Sassy was whining and scratching the carpet as if she wanted to dig her way out, seeming to sense something was wrong. Dean led Ryder inside their bedroom and had him sit on the bed. Sassy jumped up and immediately snuggled into his side. Dean and Ryder both petted her to calm her down. When she had settled, her head in Ryder's lap, Dean focused back on Ryder's leg. He knew that one of the biggest risks and setbacks to recovery would be a fall. *Damn, Bentley, I want to kill him.* "Lemme check, babe. Just to make sure. Does it hurt?"

Ryder stretched out his leg, helping Dean remove the prosthesis and sock. "A little," he said truthfully, rubbing his thigh. "Right here, might have twisted it."

"Ice pack?" Dean knelt at his feet and moved Ryder's hand away. He kneaded the sore muscle with his fingers as he looked for signs of swelling or injury. Ryder let out a soft sigh, the pain in his eyes receding.

"Nah, I think it's fine. I just stood for too long earlier and then that happened..."

Continuing the massage, Dean was still concerned. "If you had fallen, damn it. My heart stopped when I saw you lose your balance."

"I know. Scared me too." Ryder ran his fingers through Dean's hair. "But you caught me, babe."

Leaning up for a kiss, Dean softly said, "Of course I did."

"Did you hear what he said?"

"No, not all of it, but I'm sure it'll just make me want to kick his ass even more."

Ryder told him everything, voice cracking as Bentley had used all of his insecurities against him. Dean grew angrier, wanting to go after Bentley, as a red hot rage filled him. How dare he say things like that? How dare he try to hurt and manipulate Ryder? It was unacceptable. Ryder had come so far, he was healing. Dean wasn't about to let his recovery be set back because of that asshole. So he pushed away his upset, took a calming breath and moved to sit beside Ryder, placing his hand on Ryder's leg. "You know that was all BS, yeah?"

"Yeah." Ryder rested his head on Dean's shoulder. "It's like you said, he's miserable so he wants me to be too. He can't stand that I'm happy."

"Exactly, and he regrets letting you go, Ry. You are a prize, he knows that. That's why he's so pissed off."

"Well, screw him." Ryder put his arms around Dean. "I'm done with him. I'm done with his crap. He comes around again I'll get a restraining order." He kissed Dean's free hand. "Just be careful, yeah? I..."

"What?"

"He wasn't just being a dick with that last comment. I'm worried he will come after you."

"Well, I may be a teacher but you know I can hold my own." Dean kissed Ryder's temple. "I've also got General Heeler's number so if he screws with me it'll be the last thing he does."

Ryder cracked a smile. "No one should ever underestimate you."

"Damn right." Dean glanced down at Ryder's leg. "You up for going back to the party? I could just tell everyone to go home."

"Nah. Let's go enjoy the rest of the night."

"Just promise you'll take it easy?" Dean cupped Ryder's cheek and locked gazes with him. "Don't be a tough guy, I don't want you hurting."

"I will, promise." Ryder closed the distance and brushed their lips together. "It's not hurting now."

"Good." Dean slid down and helped Ryder with his prosthesis. He then stood and held out his hand. "C'mon, I'll get us some beers."

Chapter Twenty-One

Classes started in the fall and, though he was late in starting college, Ryder found he enjoyed his studies. He struggled a bit with essay writing but luckily for him, his boyfriend was a teacher who was more than willing to help when needed.

As the weather cooled, he and Dean started taking walks, then eventually short hikes. Ryder gradually built up his strength and soon could jog and even run a little. He was proud of the progress he was making. He'd even learned to drive again.

They didn't hear from Bentley after Ryder blocked his number and cut off all contact, which was a relief. He kept waiting for the other shoe to drop, though. He worried that Bentley would do something rash and that terrified him. Bentley never took rejection well.

On a Saturday afternoon, there was a knock on the door and Ryder answered, surprised to see a woman who so closely resembled his lover he had to believe she was his mother. Her dark hair was braided simply, and she was dressed in a plain skirt and white-collared shirt with a shawl. She had Dean's eyes but hers weren't full of warmth. Instead they were cold and dull. She scrunched up her nose at him.

"Is Dean home?"

What could she possibly want with Dean after all these years? Ryder stepped out onto the porch. "I'm not sure if that's a good idea, ma'am."

"And you are?" she huffed, raising her eyebrow at him.

"Ryder, ma'am. His partner."

Hand to her chest, she gasped. "You live together?"

"Yes, ma'am."

Eyes filled with sadness, she shook her head. "I told myself I would ignore this. I merely came to deliver a message and ask Dean if he'll come." She clutched a cross around her neck. "Greg, my husband, is dying of liver failure. He has asked Dean to come see him."

"You won't even call him your son and you expect him to come?" Ryder said in disbelief.

"No son of mine would lead this lifestyle." She waved at him in obvious disgust. "Yet, Greg insists upon it. He hopes Dean will see the light. He is dying and wishes to save him before he does, so please tell him to come out."

"I'll do no such thing." Ryder barred the door. "You both can go to hell. So you go tell Greg that and let him know, despite all the damage you two did, despite you throwing him out and disowning him, despite it all, Dean found a better family and a life. He is an amazing man. One you should be damned proud of. And he doesn't need saving. In fact he doesn't need anything you have to offer. I'm going to ask you to go now and not darken our door again. If there's one thing I can't stand, it's ignorant people like yourself who can't even see that God would never be so cruel and do the things you did."

"How dare you!" she bristled. "You have no right!"

"I have every right. I'm Dean's partner, I love him. I accept him for who he is and I'm here for him." Ryder took a calming breath. "I'm protecting him now. You don't get to hurt him again. Not while I'm around."

She clenched her fists and spun on her heel. "I'll be back."

"I'll call the cops," he retorted.

She stormed away. As she got to the fence, Dean, to Ryder's surprise, stepped outside and stood next to him. "Abigail, be sure to tell Greg I'll have a drink for him tonight." He muttered under his breath, "Bastard got what he deserved. Drinking like a damned fish."

Abigail's eyes widened in shock. "I knew this was a

mistake, just like you! God will punish you for this. You'll see."

Dean flinched slightly, likely from a bad memory. Ryder slid an arm around his waist then waved. "You have a nice day too, ma'am."

Abigail let out a cry of outrage, slamming the gate. Dean chuckled. "I've never seen her look like she's going to blow a gasket, you handled that so well." He sighed and turned to Ryder. "I'm glad I didn't have to."

"How much did you hear?"

"All of it." Dean rested his head on Ryder's shoulder. "I thought about not coming out here at all but then I wanted her to know you were right and I agreed with you. I don't need that hate or crap in my life."

"No, you don't." Ryder drew him into a loose embrace, kissing his hair.

"Wait until I tell Mama."

"Oh I wouldn't want to be Abigail."

That got Dean to chuckle a little. "I don't know why she even bothered. Although she did always obey Greg even when she shouldn't have."

"She fears him?" Ryder guessed.

"That's some of it. He is a mean drunk..." Dean sighed. "But he can rot in hell for all I care." He pulled back a little. "I'm going to go for a walk. Clear my head a little... I... Seeing her is bringing up a lot of bad memories."

Ryder tugged him back into his embrace. "We can go for a walk. Or we can go in and watch a movie. Or I can find other ways to distract you..."

"I don't really want to talk about it."

"You don't have to." He cupped Dean's cheek. "Just don't pull away, I know all about parents and bad memories. But that's the past. So let's leave it there and get back to having our quiet night in."

Dean leaned into the touch. "You're right. They ruined enough of my life, they don't get to bring me down anymore."

"And if she comes around again, I'll take care of it," Ryder assured.

* * * *

Dean was quiet the rest of the night and even woke later to a nightmare. Ryder held him close through it all, wishing he could help in some way. He had a feeling that Dean hadn't told him the whole story and it worried him.

So when Dean left for work, he did what he thought he had to. He called Beth and told her how Abigail had visited and that Greg was sick. He also mentioned how shaken up Dean was.

"I know he's keeping something from me," Ryder admitted. "I don't know why but I can't help him if he does."

"He should tell you himself," Beth said softly. "I'll make sure Abigail doesn't bother him again, don't worry about it."

"It has to do with him getting kicked out of their house, right? It was worse than he told me," Ryder said in understanding.

"What did he tell you?"

"That his parents saw him being gay a sin and when he couldn't hide anymore they kicked him out on the streets. Turned their back on him…" Ryder dreaded hearing what Beth had to say in response to that.

She sighed. "I shouldn't tell you this, but I know you love my son and if anyone can get him to finally see none of it was his fault, it would be you… I don't even know the whole story, not really. Just the aftermath. A broken rib, a sprained wrist, fractured cheekbone. Those were the worst of the injuries that bastard Greg inflicted on him while Abigail watched. I was a foster mom so I got custody of Dean pretty easy. It always scares me to think what could've happened if he hadn't run away afterward and had Dax find him."

A mixture of anger and sadness had Ryder choking up — he wanted to find Greg and have him answer for what he had done to Dean. "Did he go to jail?"

"Not long enough," Beth said with a bitter edge to her voice.

"Son of a bitch," he muttered then apologized for the cursing but Beth told him there was no need.

"Listen, Ryder, you know Dean has a good heart. Don't let him go to that hospital. Greg will just manipulate and hurt him again. I don't want him going through any more pain because of them."

"You don't have to worry, Beth. I won't be letting them anywhere near Dean again."

"Good. You have him call me later. Meantime, this mama bear is going to handle some things."

Ryder chuckled. "You got it, Mama."

* * * *

It was a brisk night but they went for a walk with Sassy anyway — through the park to a small pond. The stars were bright in the night sky. Ryder had suggested it and Dean was glad he had, the air helped him clear his head. His thoughts were all jumbled, emotions were bottling up. On one hand, he wanted to visit Greg and say all he had wanted to for so many years. Tell him how much better off the world would be without him. On the other, there was his mother and her Bible verses about how he should be a dutiful son and turn the other cheek. Yet his father had beaten him for being himself. And he couldn't believe in the twisted words of his mother. God was love, wasn't he? Why would God punish him when he had made him this way? And he thought God would be happy that he had found love, real honest to goodness love, with Ryder. So then he went back to seeing them again just to show them how wrong they were.

"Talk to me," Ryder whispered, slipping his hand into

Dean's as they walked along a path. Sassy stopped to sniff a bush and scratch at the grass so they paused. "Please?"

Dean stared at the sky. "I know Mama told you. What more is there to say?"

Ryder was silent for a moment. "I only asked her because you wouldn't tell me, Dean. Why won't you? You've helped me through so much and now I have a chance to do something for you and... Don't you trust me?"

Dean whipped his head around. The moon was bright and Ryder's face was illuminated in the glow. "Of course I do." He released his hold on the retractable leash so that Sassy could explore further while he and Ryder talked. He wrapped himself around Ryder, burying his face in his neck. "I just feel ashamed."

Ryder rubbed his back. "There's no reason to feel that way. You didn't do anything wrong."

He knew that now, but the teenage version of him hadn't. "I had this crush on a boy. I was young and stupid, I invited him over to play video games and he actually kissed me when I told him I liked him. Abigail caught us and started ranting stupid Bible verses at me. I had Stevie leave before Greg came home, drunk as usual. Abigail told him, he asked me and I admitted it. Dumb on my part, but I was so sick of hiding."

Dean closed his eyes but that made the horrors of that day even more real. He opened them back up and gripped Ryder a little tighter, grateful when his partner kissed his hair and held on just as tightly. "He started hitting me with his fists... I remember falling to the floor, begging him to stop, as he shouted that I was wrong and spat obscenities at me... He kicked me, said he had no son and then he just left me there." He shuddered and took a deep breath. "I thought he was going to kill me."

"Oh my God, baby." Ryder's voice hitched as he pulled back then cupped Dean's face in his hands. He wiped away an errant tear from Dean's cheek. "I'm so sorry... If he wasn't already dying..."

"I should've stopped him," Dean said, voice rough with more unshed tears. "But I was so scared and shocked that I just froze and took all his anger. And Abigail... She just watched... Afterward they threw me out in the yard. That night I snuck in to get my stuff and then ran away. I refused to let it happen again. I knew it would if I didn't leave."

"You've got nothing to be ashamed of. It makes me so angry to know he hurt you. I'm relieved that you ran away... Damn it, he could've..."

"I know." Dean doubted he could keep it together while he was this emotionally drained. He'd rather it happen in their bed, their sanctuary where he was safe and loved. Not here in the middle of a park. "Please, Ry, can we go home now?" He swiped at his eyes to stop the tears before they could fall.

"Yeah." Ryder brushed their lips together, a tender kiss of comfort and affection. "I don't want you worrying about it anymore. I know you've been thinking about going to the hospital."

"How did you know?"

Ryder just gazed at him in understanding. Dean shouldn't have been surprised, Ryder knew him better than anyone. "They're the ones who should be ashamed. You know the reason he asked for you is because he feels guilty and he should. What they did is unforgivable."

"I know it is. I don't ever want to see either of them again," Dean admitted. "It just brought everything back up and all that twisted thinking..." He rested his forehead against Ryder's. "Can we just have a weekend getaway and leave it all behind?"

"I'll pack tonight. You decide where you want to go," Ryder said without hesitation.

Dean fell in love with Ryder just a little more at that. He was so lucky to have him. He let go of his dark past and focused instead on his future, his heaven, standing right in front of him. "What would I do without you?"

"You'll never find out," Ryder assured with another kiss.

Chapter Twenty-Two

They drove out of town, found a B & B, and had an enjoyable and relaxing weekend. That was until they got back and Beth called to ask them to come over. They didn't have much time before Dean had to go to work. Still, she said it was important so they went to her house.

"What's going on, Mama?" Dean asked as she led them to the kitchen and gave them coffee that she had already made. They sat down together at the dining room table. Beth seemed calm, though Ryder had no doubt from the quiet fury in her gaze that there was going to be hell to pay for those who had crossed her and her family. He made a note to never get on her bad side.

"I heard from a friend that Abigail is up to no good. Apparently she and the women of her church are going to protest you being a gay teacher if you don't do as she wishes." Beth sighed and squeezed Dean's arm.

Dean slammed his fist on the table. "I work at a public school, they can't fire me."

"No, sweetheart, I don't think they can. Though if she goes forward you'll be thrown into the media and they'll hound you. You know it'll be big news and I don't think you want to go through that."

"Damn it." Ryder took Dean's hand.

"So what, Mama?" Dean asked. "Do I give in? Do I go against everything I am and lie to get her to stop? What if she does it anyway just to ruin my life?"

"I'm not going to let that happen," Ryder assured. "We'll figure something out."

"Oh I've got that covered." Beth took a sip from her mug.

"I just wanted you to know before I go ahead."

Dean raised an eyebrow. "What?"

"She wants to play nasty—I can too. Though I don't like it." Beth leaned forward in her chair. She sighed deeply. "She's not the pious woman she claims to be. Before she married Greg—a marriage set up by her father—she was in love with my cousin. He got her pregnant and she 'miscarried' and pretended it all never happened. Now, how do you think Greg will react to that?"

Dean ran a hand through his hand. "Jesus."

Ryder put an arm around Dean, he was clearly shocked. So was he for that matter. "You think that'll keep her quiet?"

Beth nodded. "Greg would make sure she lost everything. Let's give her a taste of her own medicine, huh?" She picked up her cell and it was only a matter of minutes before Ryder heard Abigail screaming after Beth gave her the ultimatum.

"You can't do that! You have no proof."

"Benji assures me that he has it. And if that's not enough, Stacey works at the hospital and owes me a favor. Shouldn't be too hard to dig up a few records," Beth threatened.

"You'd destroy me?" Abigail asked. "I'd never be able to go to church again. Greg's family would take away everything!"

"I can easily forget if you do. You forget again that you ever pretended to be a mother and I'll make sure your secret stays a secret."

"Why do this for him? He's a sodomite!"

Dean flinched, but Beth reached over and squeezed his hand. Ryder wanted to say something until Beth shook her head at him, letting him know she had it handled. "Say that again and I swear I will spread your story all over town and all over the net, too. You'll never escape it." She paused. "You don't have true faith or love in your heart, you have hate. Yet, God will judge you for that, as He is the only one who can."

"What am I going to tell Greg?"

"That neither of you need to bother *my* son. He's a stranger to you. Not of your concern and it's better to leave things as they are. You've lost him and that is your mistake, not his."

There was silence for a moment. "Fine, I will urge my church not to protest, though they might of their own accord."

"No, they won't. You put the idea there, you shut it down. Promise me I won't hear a word of this again. If I do, I will let everyone know how false your image is. Got it?"

"I promise, I will make certain it goes no further."

"And you'll leave Dean alone. No visits or calls, or he'll get a restraining order," Beth told her and Dean nodded. "You might have covered it up but the records are there of your abuse."

"Fine, I will have no further contact."

"Good, then we're done talking." Beth hung up. "Problem solved."

Dean got up and went around the table. He hugged her tightly. "I'm lucky to have you, Mama. And I'll never get on your bad side."

She chuckled. "You always were smart." She cupped his chin. "You are my son. I love you. Don't you ever forget that."

Dean smiled. "I won't."

Relieved that Dean no longer had to worry, Ryder reached over and squeezed his hand. "You'd better get going, baby. You don't want to be late."

Dean glanced at his watch. "Crap, you're right. I'll see you both later." He gave Ryder a kiss then dashed out of the door after grabbing his suit jacket and messenger bag.

Beth shared a look with him. "You know he's still going to end up going to see him?"

Ryder sighed. "Yep, I just want to be there when he does. I figure he needs the closure."

* * * *

Later that afternoon, Dean was grading papers and

waiting for his students to arrive for their weekly meeting during lunch. The Gay-Straight Alliance was steadily growing and his goal was to make the students feel safer and more comfortable at school. He didn't want them living in fear like he had.

Nick came into his classroom. He was an intelligent kid — quiet and often overlooked by his fellow students. He wasn't bullied so much as left out. It's why he'd suggested for him to join a few clubs. Nick was now flourishing as one of the backstage crew for the current school play. And Dean was glad to see it. "Hey, Nick. Meeting's not for another ten minutes."

As he brushed back the blond fringe from his eyes, Nick nodded. "I know, but, Mr. Anders, I needed to talk to you."

"Is everything all right?" Dean put his pen down and walked around the desk, before sitting on the edge of it.

Nick dropped his backpack on one of the chairs. "Yeah... I... I'm gay," he whispered.

Not quite a surprise but Dean sensed this was a big moment for Nick. "Am I the first person you told that to, Nick?"

"Yes." Nick ducked his head. "I felt safest telling you."

"Well, I'm honored that you confided in me. My classroom door is always open if you ever need to talk. And, Nick?" He waited until Nick looked up. "It's okay. You're not alone. Believe me when I say I know this isn't going to be easy but it honestly does get better."

Nick almost smiled. "I'm just scared of telling my old man."

"Why? Has he given you reason to be?"

Nick sat at one of the desks. "He works on base, yanno? He went on and on about how they shouldn't have gotten rid of Don't Ask, Don't Tell." He clenched his jaw. "It wasn't good."

"What about your mom?"

"I think she'd be okay." Nick shrugged. "I'm not sure."

"So, do you want to tell them?"

"Do you think I should?"

Dean knew Nick just wanted advice but he didn't want to sway or push him. Nick had to do this at his own pace, be comfortable and ready to come out. "That has to be your decision. It's up to you if you do or don't. I'm not going to judge either way."

With a bob of his head, Nick asked, "In group you said you came out at sixteen. Were your parents cool?"

"Truthfully, no. They kicked me out and I moved in with a friend who became family," Dean told him, wanting to be honest.

"If mine do that I got nowhere to go," Nick replied, biting his lip.

"No other relatives? Siblings?" Dean suggested.

"I got an aunt in California who might take me in but that'd suck to move."

"You don't have to decide today — take your time. When you're ready you'll know."

Nick locked gazes with him. "Do you regret it?"

Dean folded his hands together. "Not at all. I was done hiding. And I ended up with a family who loves me for who I am. I'm proud of all I've done, who I am."

"Cool." Nick brushed his fringe back again. "I don't want to hide, Mr. Anders. I just wanna be me without this big secret."

"I understand." Dean smiled. "You have my support. You're gay. I'm gay. The sky is blue." Nick chuckled, which was what Dean was going for. "See? No big deal."

"I hope my parents see it that way." Nick sighed.

"I do too. Let's think positively, yeah?"

"Yeah, I already feel better."

"Good." Dean glanced over as more students came to the door. "Keep me posted and remember you're not alone."

Nick stood and held out his hand for a fist bump. Dean shook his head but did it anyway. "Thanks, Mr. Anders. I'm real lucky to have you as my teacher."

Dean was touched. He knew then that he had something

he needed to do. "You're welcome, Nick. I'm proud to be your teacher."

* * * *

After school, Dean texted Ryder that he'd be home a little later than usual. He then drove to the hospital. He thought about slipping on a hoodie and going incognito but then thought, screw it. If he saw Abigail he'd just leave. He wasn't here for her. He was here to have closure, close this chapter on his past. Let it all go, like Ryder said, so he could move forward. This was his last chance to say his piece to Greg.

Luckily, one of the nurses had a daughter in his class and pointed him to the right room. Abigail wasn't there, thank goodness. Greg was a husk of the giant he'd been, with yellowish skin and thinned black hair. His hazy, drugged green eyes regarded him as he entered. He couldn't speak with the tube down his throat. Dean walked to the foot of the bed. He didn't say anything for a moment. Here was the monster of his childhood, defeated. Nothing more than an ill man.

"I thought about not coming," he started. "Then I thought it was time to say my version of farewell. So, here goes. I was unlucky enough to be born into a family that never treated me right, but I found my own family. One that loves me just the way I am. I have Beth—she knows what it means to be a parent. I had a brother, Dax. I'm going to miss him every day for the rest of my life. You..." He paused. "I'm not going to think about you once I leave." Greg raised a feeble hand. "I'm gay, not wrong. Not any of the vile words you called me. You tried to ruin me, but you were wrong about everything you told me. I have a successful career, a home, a family. I even have a man I love more than life who I definitely plan to marry someday." He folded his arms as Greg glared. "I'm going to have kids too. Probably adopt, I know you're not the only crap parent out there. I know just what not to do. I'll be a good dad and love my children unconditionally." He locked gazes with Greg. "I just wanted you to know I'm happy and loved, so no, I don't forgive you, but thank you for kicking me out. It was the one thing you ever did right for me." He turned on his heel and left the room. He felt a weight lift, footsteps lighter as he walked out of the hospital to his car.

His breath caught as he saw Ryder leaning against it, wearing his ball cap, shirt and jeans with the sun setting behind him. Damn, he wasn't sappy but it really was a gorgeous sight. He ran over and threw his arms around Ryder's neck, kissing him.

Ryder rested his hand on the small of his back. "Hey, baby."

"Hey, how did you know I'd be here? I didn't even know until this afternoon."

"You needed closure," Ryder said. "I just wanted to be here in case you needed me."

Dean filled him in and told him what he'd said. Well, mostly. It was too soon to bring up marriage, but there was no doubt in his mind. Ryder was the one. Him being here, waiting, only proved it again. He was always there when Dean needed him, and at the same time he'd stepped back and let him handle it on his own. It was a comfort knowing that if it hadn't gone so well Ryder would've been there to make it better. "I'm glad you're here." He kissed Ryder again because he could. He was lucky and feeling grateful. "Let's go out to dinner. You hungry?"

Ryder rubbed his back. He nipped Dean's lip. "Not really. For food anyway."

"Mm, I like the way you think." Dean pressed into him. "Takeaway?"

"Now you're talking." Ryder grinned. "Keys?"

Dean fished them out of his pocket. "Wait, how'd you get here?"

"Jessie. I was going to drive myself, get some practice. But I wanted to drive home with you."

Ryder had thought of everything. Dean smiled. "I love you, Ry."

Cupping his cheek, Ryder brushed their lips together. "I love you, too." He paused. "I'm glad you got closure. It'll help."

"Yep, the past is in the past." He met Ryder's gaze. "I'm only looking forward now."

Chapter Twenty-Three

Months passed by, autumn turning to winter. Ryder worked on his degree while continuing rehab. It wasn't long before he could do everything he used to. Everything he had thought impossible just a few months before. And he owed it to Dean. When he was tired, sore and ready to throw in the towel, Dean was there to pick him up and keep him going.

When Ryder had ironed out all the details for their trip to Washington, DC in March, to receive his medal, he had made sure that he and Dean would have a romantic getaway. Just a small way to show him how much he loved and appreciated him. Then he had an even better idea. He headed to the mall to Kay's Jewelers. He called up Beth before going inside.

"Hi, B—Mama," he said, his nerves making his stomach feel like it was full of butterflies. "I, uh, wanted to talk to you about something."

"What is it, honey?"

Here it goes. "I... I want to propose to Dean." Ryder ran a hand through his hair. "Before you say anything, please let me say this. I love him, Beth. I mean really, the kind of love a guy like me thought I'd never have. And I know we've only been actually together for four months but life is so damn short. I learned that, I learned what's important too. Having Dean pull me up from rock bottom and make my life worth living again... He's amazing. And I never want to let him go..."

"Ryder," Beth said, and he could tell she was crying.

"I want your blessing, Beth," he continued on. "You're

Dean's family and I want to know I have your support."

"Of course you do! Nothing would make me happier than to have you and Dean get married," Beth said. Now he could hear a smile in her voice. "Go on, sweetheart. You mean the world to my son and you both deserve happiness. When are you going to propose? I'd love to be there if you wouldn't mind."

"Not at all. I was thinking since we're going to DC in a few months I'd plan something and pop the question. We can get married there."

"Oh that'll be a wonderful surprise," Beth agreed. "Let me know if you need anything."

"I will. Thanks." Ryder said goodbye, disconnected the call and stepped inside the jewelry store. It took him a while but he finally found the perfect ring. Silver titanium with an infinity loop etched into it. Feeling like he was on top of the moon, he headed home. He figured he had an hour until Dean was off work, enough time to hopefully wipe the stupid grin off his face. It wouldn't be easy to keep the secret, and it'd be even more difficult to not just ask, but he wanted to do it right. Dean deserved a grand gesture and to be swept off his feet.

* * * *

It was a chilly day — there had been a light snowfall earlier and the ground was dusted with it. Heading out to his car, one arm full of books, Dean was both annoyed and a bit worried to see Bentley casually leaning against his Saturn. He stuck a hand in his pocket, wrapping his fingers around the small Taser attached to his keychain.

"To what do I owe the privilege?"

Bentley turned his gaze to him, eyes red-rimmed. He looked like he'd had a little too much to drink. *Great.*

"I owe you an ass kicking."

After he had set the books on the hood, Dean regarded him with disdain. "You should go sleep it off."

"Nah, here's how it's gonna go. Two choices, fag. One, you call Ryder now to tell him it's over and he has to leave—"

"Like hell I will!" Dean clenched his fist.

"Fine, choice two. I kick your ass and make you tell him."

"I'd like to see you try." Bentley stepped forward and Dean raised a hand. "But before you do, let me give you *your* choices."

"Oh right, like I'm going to listen to this."

"You'll want to, believe me. We can fight, but you're not the only one Army trained. My brother always feared some ignorant bastard would come along and so he taught me how to defend myself."

"Like that's anything like fighting for your life in combat," Bentley yelled.

"No, but my life is Ry, so if I gotta fight for it, I will. I'm not ever going to let you hurt him again, you dick."

Bentley came at him, but Dean dodged and pulled out the Taser, pushing it between the other man's ribs. Bentley bent over, gasping. "Now, you know General Heeler, don't you?"

"So?"

"His daughter, Jessie. You know her?"

"No."

After he'd taken his phone from his pocket, Dean scrolled to his pictures. "Shame. Anyway, Jessie, she was engaged to my brother. We had a big party to celebrate." He briefly showed Bentley the picture of everyone gathered together. "See, I know Rudy. I have his number here." He brought up his contacts. "I'm sure he'd love to know one of his men just tried to assault me. Won't that do wonders for your precious career?"

Bentley glared at him, but Dean saw that he was shaking slightly. "You wouldn't dare."

"Try me." Dean held his thumb over the call icon.

Bentley straightened and reached into his pocket. Instinct kicked in. Dean tackled him to the ground with an 'oomph'. The gun flew out of Bentley's hand. Dean punched Bentley in the face twice before he was thrown off and kicked hard in the ribs. A sharp pain and a crack had him gasping for air. But he rolled, desperate to reach the weapon first. He had it in his grasp but Bentley stepped on his fingers and he cried out, letting go. Bones snapped and white hot pain shot from his hand. He realized how stupid he'd been to engage Bentley in a fight.

When Bentley bent down for the Glock, Dean kicked up as hard as he could. His shoe connected with Bentley's jaw, sending him flying backward. With his uninjured hand he grabbed the firearm, pointed it at Bentley and struggled to his feet.

"Move and I swear to God." Dean released the safety.

Bentley held up his hands. "Easy. You win. You sure can fight."

Dean spat blood on the pavement. He glanced around for his phone. He thought he could make a call with his other hand—it didn't feel like all of his fingers were badly broken. Keeping the gun trained on Bentley, he scooped it up. It hurt like hell but he managed to hold it. The screen had a crack but it still worked.

"Wait, you can't call the cops! I could get discharged."

"Should've thought of that. I warned you." Dean's whole body hurt, but he dialed nine-one-one. No one way he could take another round of punches. And he wasn't sure what Bentley would try, although he didn't want to shoot him.

"You don't have it in you," Bentley said a little too cockily. "And I'm not going to jail."

Dax's words came to him then. *Remember, go with your gut, little bro. Don't think—act. I know you, you need to focus on defending yourself. You don't want to hurt nobody, I get that, but that don't mean they don't want to hurt you.* He almost felt Dax at his shoulder as he fired a shot, letting it go wide. "I won't miss next time."

He heard sirens. He guessed that someone on campus must have seen the skirmish. Bentley paled and he took a step back, as if he were ready to flee.

"Don't move."

"If you let me go I swear I won't ever bother you again," Bentley pleaded.

Dean didn't buy it. "If I let you go, Ryder will hunt you down."

Rubbing his jaw, Bentley tried again. "I'm sorry, okay? I don't know what I was thinking. I'm just so angry and hurt."

"That Ryder finally moved on? Why do you even care?"

"Because I love him!" Bentley threw up his hands. "I do. And now he wants nothing to do with me. I'm alone... I just can't—"

"Admit you're gay?" Dean shook his head. "Yeah, I know the story."

"You don't know what it's like to be afraid of coming out," Bentley told him and Dean couldn't help but laugh bitterly.

"You don't know me, Bentley. I got kicked out of my parents' house for coming out when I was sixteen. I nearly got beat to death by my father. My life hasn't been easy, but unlike you I never tried to hide who I was or make the man I love deny who he is just because of what others think."

A cop car pulled up and Dean put down the weapon. Bentley was cuffed and Dean explained to the officer what had happened as a paramedic tended to him. Shaking slightly and feeling the adrenaline wearing off, Dean was grateful to lie on the gurney in the ambulance as he was taken to the hospital. The ER doctor was quick to take X-rays and give him some morphine before they splinted his two broken fingers. It all went by in a blur of activity that left him disconnected and wanting Ryder. They were ready to discharge him after that as his injuries didn't require an overnight stay. He knew how hard this was going to be for Ryder, that his partner would blame himself. But he needed him, he wanted Ryder to wrap him in his arms and make him forget all about this nightmare.

He called Ryder's cell. "Ry?"

"You're late, babe. I was starting to worry."

"About that," Dean started to say, voice catching. "I, uh, ran into Bentley."

"Oh God, are you hurt? Where are you?"

"At Mercy. Cracked rib and two broken fingers," Dean admitted.

"I'll kill the son of a bitch."

"He's in jail." Dean rubbed his temple. "Can you come get me? I'm too doped up and my car is back at school."

"I'm on my way." Ryder paused then his voice dropped, "I'm so sorry, love. So sorry."

"It's not your fault. I don't want you blaming yourself for this."

"He went after you because of me!"

"Yeah, but I'm okay, babe. Just let it go for now and get here." Dean curled up on the hospital bed.

"I'm in my truck. Won't be long."

Dean was glad that Ryder had relearned to drive and had made a few accommodations so he could. The doctor came in with papers and a prescription for pain meds so Dean told Ryder he'd see him in a few minutes and signed the paperwork. Ten minutes later, Ryder ran into the room. He had a wild-eyed look that calmed when his eyes met Dean's.

Dean got up and before he knew it he was in Ryder's strong embrace. He buried his face in his partner's neck, breathing in his scent as a few tears fell and wet his collar. Ryder murmured comforting words in his ear and rubbed soothing circles on his back.

"Tell me what happened," Ryder said quietly after a few minutes.

Dean pulled back and saw that Ryder's eyes were now filled with tears as well. Cradling Dean's injured hand in his, Ryder kissed his bruised knuckles. With all the adrenaline, Dean hadn't had a chance to be scared, but thinking back he shuddered and realized how lucky he was to only have a couple of broken fingers and a cracked rib. Ryder sat with him on the hospital bed and Dean told him everything. He saw the fury in Ryder's gaze along with his guilt as he shook his foot and bit his lip.

With a kiss to his temple, Ryder murmured, "If anything had happened to you... I don't know what I'd have done."

Dean simply held onto him. He wanted to go home and put this behind them. "It's over now, at least. He'd be stupid to bother either of us again."

Ryder pressed a kiss to his hair. "I have friends who owe me favors. I'll be sure if he isn't discharged that he gets transferred far from here."

"Good. I wasn't scared then but now..." Another shudder had him clinging to Ryder just a little tighter.

"I've got you now. Let's go home so you can rest and I can take care of you."

"Yeah, let's go home."

Chapter Twenty-Four

The ring box weighed heavily in his pocket as Ryder followed Dean inside. He watched his partner carefully. Dean put his phone and keys on the counter before going to the living room and collapsing on the couch. Sassy jumped up to greet him and cuddled close, licking his cheek then his splinted fingers. Dean petted her, rubbing her ears affectionately. His other hand was wrapped around his ribs and Ryder could tell that he was in pain. Seeing him hurt, knowing he was the cause had him feeling guilty all over again.

Dean turned his head back toward him. "Babe?"

"You hungry? How about tomato soup and grilled cheese?"

"Comfort food, yes please." Dean directed a soft smile at him then yawned. "If I fall asleep just wake me."

"It won't take me long." Ryder walked over and leaned down to kiss Dean. "Just rest and take it easy."

"I will if you stop feeling guilty."

A sigh escaped. "I can't help it. You're hurt...because of my jealous ex."

"Yeah, because of that rat bastard. Neither one of us saw this coming."

Ryder looked away. He barely had his emotions in check, the regret flooding back. He knew Bentley, he knew his temper, he should've done something before it got this far. Bentley no longer saw him as a threat so he would've been surprised and never seen it coming. Right now, Ryder wanted to strangle his former friend with his bare hands. Anger bubbled inside him—he needed to go a round at the punching bag in the gym. Instead he took a few deep calming breaths, forcing himself to get it under control. He'd deal with Bentley later. "He has a temper, he was drinking. I should've known..."

Dean raised his eyebrow. "Why, did he do something like this before? How the hell is he still in the Army if he did?"

Sitting on the arm of the couch, Ryder replied, "No. I mean, there was a bar brawl once, but we were all drunk and young and stupid."

"So again, Ry, why blame yourself?" Dean asked quietly.

"Because I break everything I touch!" Ryder stood and left the room. He felt himself spiraling as he suddenly remembered the last words his mother had ever spoken to him before she'd abandoned him. It was true, too, he couldn't ever be happy. He kept trying but he didn't deserve it. Eventually, he feared, Dean would see that and leave him. He was kidding himself buying a ring. Why would he want to commit to a broken man who ruined everything? His vision became blurry with tears he refused to let fall.

"Ryder, talk to me," Dean pleaded, coming up behind him. "What do you mean by that?"

"I mean just what I said..." Ryder stared out of the window, crossing his arms. "I was five, I barely remember it but... My mother dropped me off at that firehouse after her latest boyfriend left. I knew she was sad so I tried to cheer her up but I screwed up instead." He closed his eyes. It wasn't much he had done wrong. A broken wine glass but it was the last straw for his mother and he told Dean as much. "The next day she was so happy and it was because she got rid of me..."

"Ry..." Dean's voice cracked.

"It's the reason why I've never been good enough, not for any of those foster families, not for anyone..." Ryder hung his head. "I thought maybe I had finally gotten over this curse, that maybe they were all wrong. Or at the very least I had suffered enough with my leg. And then this happened. You're hurt." He could barely speak—the lump in his throat grew bigger. "He could've— And it would've been because of me. Because you love me and I don't deserve it. You do deserve better, though and I don't want you hurt any—"

"Then don't you dare say those words!" Dean spun him around, nearly catching him off balance. "I do love you. And you can push, and you can feel guilty, and Bentley can come at me again, and I still won't leave. I'm *not* abandoning you, Ry." He locked gazes with him and cupped Ryder's face, not allowing him to look away. "I'm not running away because things got tough. I can handle it. You gotta trust that and see that they were wrong. That the only way you break that curse you think you got is by letting all that hurt in your past go. Just like I did. Let it go, babe, and see that I'm right here." He pressed a kiss to Ryder's temple. "You didn't break anything. I'm fine. And we're okay."

Ryder put his hand over Dean's broken fingers. He strangled a sob back as he stared at Dean. A burden he hadn't even realized he'd had lifted with those words. He hadn't hurt Dean, he hadn't broken their relationship. There was still hope. If he could just let go like Dean said. Then he truly thought about it—his mother had abandoned him for her party lifestyle. He hadn't done anything wrong. The foster families had just been temporary and the wrong fit, it wasn't his fault that he had got stuck with the worst of the bunch. And Bentley, yes, he had made a mistake with him, but he had left and gotten his life together. He'd lived out and proud in the military, made a sacrifice for his country, and found love when he had gotten home. Real honest to God love, from a man who didn't even realize every day how he healed the brokenness inside him with a kiss and three little words. He wasn't cursed, not anymore. All he had to do was make certain that no one ever hurt Dean again and show him just how lucky he was to have his adoration. All he had to do was hold onto Dean.

He buried his face in Dean's neck, wrapping him gently in his arms as he let go. Tears fell, releasing all the hurt that had built up over all his life. Dean murmured in his ear and held on, letting him cry and easing away the hurt. "I've got you, Ry," he whispered.

Feeling drained but better, Ryder pulled back and swiped at his eyes. Dean fought a yawn.

"You're tired. I'm sorry for breaking down. I didn't... I don't cry, not usually."

Dean pressed a finger to his lips. "It's all right. Sometimes things like that just hit you. You saw how hard it was for me learning about Greg. But you helped me see none of it was my fault, that if I held onto the hurt and bitterness it'd eat away at me. So I let go, and I stopped worrying about what could've been and focused instead on what I have and what I need to be happy."

"You're right about everything, baby. I know I don't need much. But I do need you. That's all I need to be happy."

Dean broke into a smile and kissed him. "Good, because that's all I need."

Ryder deepened the kiss for just a moment, losing himself in how good it felt. "Why don't you go rest in bed and I'll bring the food in," he said against Dean's lips. "We can watch a movie and if you fall asleep it'll be more comfortable."

"I like the way you think."

Ryder kissed him again, just because he could, then he let Dean go lie down as he grilled the sandwiches and made soup. Dean's phone started ringing when he was halfway through, and when he saw it was Rudy, he grabbed it.

"Hello, sir," he answered.

"Ryder, I called to check on Dean. How is he?"

"Resting, sir. I was just making dinner."

"The report says a cracked rib and two broken fingers."

"Yes, sir."

"I've had Mathers court marshaled for a nine twenty and a nine twenty-eight—stalking and assault. He's been detained. You can assure Dean that I've taken care of matters."

"Thank you, sir. I will let him know."

"Off the record, Mathers is saying you repeatedly tried to

143

seduce him, though he's claiming he's straight. I found that difficult to believe when he couldn't explain why he went to see Dean. He tried saying as well that Dean attacked him, but I don't buy it as he clearly stalked him and had his weapon."

Ryder pinched the bridge of his nose. "We haven't had more than a professional relationship for years. He wouldn't admit he's gay and is still denying it. I cut ties but then he saved my life and he was there, which I appreciated. Then things got ugly when he saw how Dean and I clicked. He tried to start a fight once before and made threats but that was a while ago and I had hoped he'd let it go. That was stupid on my part."

"Do you have witnesses to this previous argument?"

"Specialist Cruz was there, yes."

"I may need to talk to him. It sounds very clear to me," Rudy replied. "I'm going to recommend rehab and then the court can decide what to do with him. I suggest you get a restraining order, too, though if he bothers you again, I'll make sure he does serious jail time."

"Yes, sir. I'll go down to the station."

"Good, I'll be in touch. I'll need both your testimonies."

"Of course. Thank you, sir."

"You did a service for this country, son. It's only fair that we have your back. And Dean is like family—no one messes with family."

"Agreed."

"You have a good night."

"You too, sir."

Ryder finished making dinner after disconnecting the call. Now, Dean needed him, and still wanted him despite what had happened, so he had to make sure he knew that he was all that mattered to him in this world. And hope like hell that Dean would still say yes when he asked him. Not now, not with this hanging over them. He wanted it to be a memory that would last forever and not be tainted by this horrible day.

* * * *

The next morning Dean decided to call in sick. There was no way he could teach with his whole body aching. Ryder gave him some pain meds and his phone before getting back into bed with him. Dean called Jeannie, the principal, and filled her in. "I just need a few days to heal, Jeannie, then I'll be fine."

"Of course, take all the time you need. I can get a sub for a week if you need it." She paused. "I don't want the students panicking or parents freaking out so would you agree to say you were just in a minor accident?"

"I understand, I don't want them scared either. It was just one idiot and he's locked up so there's no reason to concern them."

"Agreed, and I'm so sorry you were hurt, Dean. You're one of my best teachers, and the kids love you. I'm glad you're all right."

"Thanks."

"You're welcome. I've gotta run, but you take care and get better, y'hear?"

"Yes, ma'am."

Dean hung up. Ryder took the phone then kissed him. "So, Netflix marathon after I make us breakfast? French toast?"

"You've got class."

"Just a lecture, I'll get notes from someone." Ryder shrugged. "I'm staying here and taking care of you."

Dean was content snuggled up next to him. "Okay, well in that case, I'm still a little tired. Can we stay like this for a bit?"

"For as long as you want." Ryder drew him closer and stroked his hair, soothing him.

He'd dozed off until he heard the doorbell. Ryder kissed his temple and started to sit up. Dean realized he'd need a few minutes so he thought about getting up as well until he heard the front door open.

"Dean!" Beth called out frantically. Sassy barked excitedly and dashed out to greet her.

Dean got up too fast, ribs screaming in protest, but he shared a look with Ryder then headed out of the room. His mom was already in the hall. Tears in her eyes, she rushed forward and embraced him. It hurt but she was shaking so he returned the hug.

After a few moments, she calmed and pulled away. "Dean Russell Anders, why didn't you call me? Rudy rang to check in and I about had a heart attack!"

"I'm sorry, Mama. Ryder took me home from the hospital and we got here and I just crashed."

"I should've called," Ryder apologized from the doorway. "I'm sorry, Beth, for worrying you."

She shook her head, fighting back tears. "It's just… There is no greater pain than losing your child. I'm barely hanging on after Dax," she whispered. "Here I was thinking at least you were safe here and then…" She trailed off with a strangled sob.

Dean pulled her into his arms again, kissing the top of her head. "I'm fine, Mama. Really. Just some bruises and broken fingers."

"Don't you lie, Dean. A man pulled a gun on you!"

"I stopped him, though," Dean tried to reassure her. He could tell how scared she was and he wanted to take away her hurt. He knew he couldn't—there was a Dax-sized hole in his heart, too, but he was still here. He could give her that comfort at least. "I'm not going to let anything take me away from you or Ry."

She cried into his chest. He held her tightly. He glanced over to see Ryder hanging his head. He gestured him over and put his free arm around Ryder, drawing him into the embrace. He wasn't about to have him feeling guilty again. The only one who had to answer for this was Bentley and he knew Rudy would take care of things.

After a few minutes, Beth's sobs subsided. She pulled back, wiping away her tears. "Never scare me like that again, you hear?"

Dean gave her a small smile. "Yes, Mama."

"How about breakfast?" Ryder offered.

"We were going to make French toast," Dean added.

"If you don't mind." Beth gave them a watery smile. She scooped up Sassy, who was begging for attention, and cuddled her.

"We never do," Ryder told her, walking away to the kitchen. Beth followed.

"Ryder, wait," Beth said and he turned to her.

"I don't blame you for this." Beth's voice was soft. "You can no more control another man's actions than you can the weather."

Relief filled Ryder's features. "I... I was blaming myself last night until Dean and I talked. I still would never have forgiven myself if..."

Dean stepped over and cupped Ryder's face, brushing their lips together. "None of that. Like I said, nothing is going to come between us."

"Yeah, I'm the luckiest guy ever to have you."

"Yep, and so am I." Dean kissed him again. Time for a change in subject, he wanted to lighten the mood and turn it to happier topics. "Now, food. I'm hungry."

"You wanna start the coffee?"

Beth took a seat at the table with the morning paper as Dean made coffee and Ryder started making his famous French toast. Ryder's phone rang and Dean took over, dipping bread in the mixture.

"Joel?" Ryder listened intently. "Yeah, you gotta get in line... I appreciate that. Yeah, he's okay... Yep, that works... All right, I'll talk to you soon."

Ryder disconnected the call. He added butter to a skillet. "The squad all want to kick Bentley's ass. Joel is going to give a statement."

"Well, that's good." Dean placed the bread in the pan. He stepped back and went to the fridge for the syrup and blueberries. "I know we gotta give statements but I'm not going to think about it now."

Ryder flipped the toast. After the other side was browned, he slid it on a plate. Dean was going to add syrup but Ryder grabbed his phone and a song started playing. He grinned and winked at Dean. Raising an eyebrow, Dean wondered what he was up to.

"I know how to take your mind off things." He took Dean's hand and put the other on the small of his back. "All of me loves all of you," he sang. Ryder was a beautiful singer, voice like honey as they swayed to the music. Breakfast and all their troubles forgotten, Dean rested his head on Ryder's shoulder, content to be led around the kitchen. He smiled and sang along to the chorus. *Yep, even when I lose, I'm winning. Because I have Ryder.*

Chapter Twenty-Five

A week before Christmas, during winter break, they took their planned vacation to Wolf Ridge. They rented a cabin where they intended to stay until the day after Christmas. Beth was visiting her brother Eric and Jessie was watching Sassy. Everything was settled for them to get away together. It was snowing as Dean drove their rented Explorer up to their cabin.

The cabin was spacious. When they walked through the entryway the first floor was laid out before them in a wide open space. In the lounge area a leather sofa and recliner were situated near a huge stone fireplace. In the opposite corner, there was a small kitchen and a table for two. A winding staircase took them up to the master bedroom with an adjoining bathroom. The tub had jets and could easily fit four men.

"Nice. Definitely going to have to try that out," Ryder said.

"Should we unpack first?" Dean teased him.

Ryder's stare was heated. "That's the last thing on my mind."

Dean went back into the bedroom. The king-sized bed had a canopy, there was another fireplace across from it, and heavy navy blue curtains covered a wall of glass. Ryder pulled them back, letting in the bright sunlight and giving them a stunning view of the snow-covered forest.

"I don't think I ever want to leave." Dean flopped back on the bed.

"Hmm, we can just stay in bed and make love forever." Ryder flashed him a cheeky grin as he stood by the window.

Propping himself up on his elbows, Dean crooked a finger. "You have the best ideas."

Ryder strode across the floor and leaned over for a kiss. Dean tugged him close, deciding that unpacking could wait. It would be much more fun to christen the cabin first.

* * * *

The next morning, Dean took Ryder's hand and led him blindfolded into the Snow Sports School. He'd done his homework with this. Planned it all out. When they had booked the cabin on Wolf Ridge, Ryder had seen the snowboarding and ski resort. He had confessed to Dean that he loved to snowboard but figured he couldn't do it anymore. Dean wasn't about to let him give up anything.

"Can I take this off now?"

"Almost." Dean clutched the board in hand that he had bought for Ryder and watched him, trying not to smile. Ryder was in for quite a surprise that he hoped he would like. "Okay, go ahead."

A redheaded instructor approached them. "Hi, I'm Mandy. Are you here for some lessons?"

Ryder removed the blindfold and stared at her in shock. "Um, Dean?"

"We are, Mandy. Could you just give us a moment, please?"

"Sure thing, let me know when you're ready." She gave them a bubbly smile before going off to greet another couple.

Ryder put his hand over the board. He stared at it, his eyes lighting up. It was Army camo printed with his name written across it. Dean had spent a bit but it was totally worth it to make Ryder happy. "What is all this?"

"A surprise." Dean was a little nervous but he smiled anyway. "I did the research, babe. You can still snowboard, no problem. Your prosthetist told me you'd be fine. I got a board that we made sure will work with it. And then I called here—they've got an adaptive instructor and they can give you lessons. You'll be flying down the slopes in no time."

"I thought I'd have to give it up," Ryder whispered, seeming at a loss for words.

Dean squeezed his hand. "Not while I'm around, you're not giving up anything."

"I can't believe you did all this." Ryder's voice caught. He pulled Dean into a hug, pressing a kiss to his hair. "I love you, so much. Thank you."

Dean's smile grew. "Anything for you. And I love you, too." He gave Ryder the board. "C'mon, let's go have some fun."

"Hell yeah!" Ryder took the board and together they joined Mandy for the lessons.

Dean had never snowboarded before so he learned right beside Ryder. They practiced and had a good time, laughing and falling, and getting back up and doing it all over again. Ryder managed to get down a small slope and Dean cheered him on, whooping as he boarded down and skidded to a stop beside him.

Ryder's lips were cold but Dean welcomed a kiss and was smiling when they broke apart. Ryder brushed some snow from his hair. "This is incredible, babe."

"I had no idea it could be so much fun," Dean agreed. "Not too tired?"

"Nah, I'm good." Ryder grinned. "You wanna race?"

"Oh really?" Dean laughed. "You're on. Winner down the next slope gets a massage tonight!"

"Mmm, sounds to me like I win either way."

* * *.*

Ryder was tempted to get down on one knee that night and ask Dean to marry him. If he had had the ring and didn't have his plans, he certainly would have. The surprise— being able to snowboard—the amazing day, it had been

151

perfect. Just when he had thought he couldn't love Dean more, he had gone and done this, making him fall even harder. Damn if he didn't have a little bit of heaven beside him.

He might have lost the race—on purpose—but he couldn't help himself. Getting to rub and touch Dean all over, massage and totally relax his lover, yeah he was loving every minute. And the sounds Dean was making, moans and sighs of pleasure, well he was so hard it hurt.

He sat back on the bed, and Dean rolled over, a lazy, content smile on his face. "Wow..."

"Let me get that fire stoked then I'll be right back," Ryder promised, stealing a kiss.

It was chilly but it wouldn't be once he added more logs to the fire. He did that, then to his surprise, Dean gently pushed him back onto the chaise. He swallowed hard as Dean settled in his lap. His knees were on either side of Ryder's hips and their bodies aligned, with their hard cocks rubbing together. Ryder worked a hand over Dean's, coating his fingers in pre-cum before offering them to his lover to suck. Dean slowly drew Ryder's fingers into his mouth, enjoying the taste of them without breaking eye contact.

He ran his other hand up Dean's smooth chest, pinching his nipples between his thumbs before Dean attacked his mouth with a passionate and needy kiss. Ryder moaned and arched into it, letting Dean control the kiss as he tried to reach for the lube that was nearby. Discarded yesterday and left on the chaise. He coated his fingers with it. He succeeded just barely and trailed them down the cleft of Dean's ass. To steady Dean, he placed his other hand on his lover's hip while he teased the puckered opening. Skin glistening with the oil in the firelight, cock erect, eyes hooded with desire, Dean was a breathtaking sight. Slowly, he eased a finger inside his lover, crooking it gently. Ryder nearly came when Dean pushed back on the digit.

"More," Dean pleaded. He tangled his fingers in Ryder's

hair while he gripped the back of the chaise with his other hand as his body undulated against Ryder.

Biting his lip and desperately holding back his own orgasm, Ryder added in a second finger as Dean relaxed and stretched around them. He slid in a third and brushed all three against Dean's prostate. Dean cried out, head thrown back.

"Ry, please. Please. Need you." Dean rode his fingers and panted. His cock was leaking now and Ryder couldn't resist, stroking, adding a twist as Dean shuddered and fought not to come, though Ryder knew he was right on the edge.

Ryder wanted inside him, *now*. He wanted to feel Dean lose control, wanted to do that to him. He pulled his fingers out. "You wanna ride me?"

"Yeah." Dean gasped. "You're overdressed, babe."

"Yeah," he croaked, grabbing Dean's face and kissing him hungrily. Dean kept grinding down. Ryder somehow managed to lift him enough to push his boxers down his thighs. "Let me take —"

"Nah, just like this," Dean breathed against his lips, reaching down to stroke Ryder's dick.

Ryder gasped but even through the fog of desire he realized he should remove the prosthesis. Shouldn't he? He had always made certain they made it to bed and he took it off before they made love. He supposed he could keep it on but he wasn't sure how he'd feel about that. A bit vulnerable, he stared at Dean, silently asking him what he wanted to do.

"You know I don't care." Dean kissed along his jaw. "Leave it. Then you'll see what I already know — it doesn't matter. We can make love either way, nothing changes." He gazed at Ryder, his affection shining through. "You're beautiful and I love you."

That decided it. He trusted Dean and suddenly didn't care either way. Dean was right, it was just them, making love and sharing this intimacy. Nothing else mattered. He knew in Dean's eyes he was beautiful. Ryder tugged him closer, kissing him again and pouring all his love into it. "Love you," he murmured over and over.

Dean quickly coated Ryder's cock with lube with an anticipatory gleam in his eye. He held onto Dean as he positioned himself over his dick and sank down. Ryder closed his eyes in pleasure as he was encased in tight heat.

Ryder leaned forward and captured Dean's lips in a gentle kiss, running his fingers through his thick black hair. "I love you, too," Dean breathed, smiling tenderly at him.

Ryder rested his hands on Dean's hips. "Ride me, baby."

"Fuck, you feel so good." Dean gripped Ryder's shoulders, rising up then slowly sinking down. Ryder loved seeing Dean rising and falling in a slow rhythm above him. He thrust up as Dean came down. Their bodies rocked together, finding a steady rhythm, and he savored the feeling of being joined and complete.

Gradually picking up the pace, Dean rode Ryder's shaft with reckless abandon, moving up and down. Ryder thought Dean looked incredibly erotic and wanton, covered in a sheen of sweat as he lost himself in how good it felt.

After grabbing the back of Dean's head, Ryder kissed him passionately. He held onto Dean's hip tightly with his other hand, while his feet were planted firmly on the ground letting him thrust up harder as Dean came down. He was glad he had more leverage so he could give Dean what he wanted. Dean began to move faster. Ryder helped him angle his descent each time so that he struck his prostate over and over. He knew the moment he had as Dean gasped and pleaded, "Harder."

"I'm so close," Dean panted. "Need to come."

Ryder could feel how close Dean was. He captured Dean's mouth with his own, swallowing his partner's moans and gasps. He snaked a hand between their bodies and found Dean's cock where it was trapped, adding even more pressure to the delicious friction he knew Dean was already enjoying. "C'mon, baby," Ryder whispered. "Lose control, let me make you fly."

"God, Ryder, I'm going to come!" Dean gasped. "So close, so good." He was panting and thrusting down, seeking to take Ryder even deeper. He dug his fingers into Ryder's shoulder and the chaise, his whole body tightening as he slipped over the edge.

"Come for me, Dean," Ryder breathed against Dean's lips. He increased the tempo of his thrusts and strokes.

Ryder swallowed his partner's cries as Dean's orgasm seized him. His cock swelled further in Ryder's grip and he came, pulsing in hot waves over Ryder's hand as he milked his release from him. Dean threw his head back, lolling from side to side. "Ry, oh my God!"

Ryder clenched Dean's waist tightly as his partner's ass contracted around his cock. He continued thrusting erratically through Dean's orgasm, feeling himself hurtled to the edge at the sight and feel of Dean in the throes of pleasure. "Dean, gonna come!" The emotions and sensations were too much—his back arched and he came, shooting deep into Dean's body with a loud shout of his partner's name.

Wrapping his arms around Dean as his lover dropped his head onto his shoulder, Ryder collapsed back onto the chaise with him. Dean burrowed his face in Ryder's neck and he sighed contently. No words were needed as they let their love wrap around them.

Slowly their breathing returned to normal and their hearts stopped pounding. Ryder felt himself slip from Dean's body and his partner whimpered at the loss. He ran his fingers tenderly through Dean's sweaty hair, pressing kisses to his face.

"Didn't hurt you, did I?"

"Nope." Dean gave him a sated smile. "How did it feel?"

"Amazing as always," he deflected and Dean swatted his arm. "All right, honestly? I didn't even think about it. I don't even know why I was being stubborn and pulling you back to the bed every time."

"Well, now you can take me wherever you want," Dean

teased, kissing his jaw. "And I'm glad you're comfortable. I didn't think about it either. Actually, I didn't think about anything. Brain's too fried for that."

Ryder chuckled. Dean was just teasing but when he thought about it, he had nixed a few attempts at lovemaking outside the bedroom, preferring the safer, more comfortable option. He didn't let doubt creep in, or a tiny voice tell him that Dean had probably gotten bored. Instead he focused on what he knew was true. Dean had just helped him through another issue that he hadn't even realized was a problem until he'd gotten past it. He ran a hand down Dean's back. "So kitchen counter, sofa, backyard swing, in front of the fireplace," he listed off. "Which part of the cabin should we have fun in next?"

Dean grinned. "Too cold outside. I like the fireplace idea." He paused. "As soon as you tell me what you were thinking that got these lines on your forehead." He rubbed them. "I'm not bored if that's what you were thinking."

Ryder couldn't help but gape at him. "I stomped down that thought," he assured.

"Good, because I was just teasing." Dean ran his fingers through his hair. "It doesn't matter how or where. Just that I get to make love to you. To share this." He grabbed Ryder's hand and pressed it to his heart. "You and me, that's all that matters."

"Damn right." Ryder could feel the steady beat under his palm. "Sometimes I limit myself without even thinking. I'm still adjusting, I guess. I'm just glad I have you to push me when I need it, so I can see I have no limits."

"Exactly." Dean kissed him tenderly. "No limits."

"I'm getting that now." Ryder smiled at him. "So what should we try next, skydiving?"

Dean chuckled. "Yeah, you might be on your own for that. How about ski mobiles?"

"Tomorrow? That'd be fun."

"Mm, not as fun as this, though." He kissed Ryder softly, hands caressing down his chest.

"Hey, you'll get no complaints from me if we stay here all day tomorrow. We could do this." He dipped Dean back and swooped in for a kiss. "We could do this." He caressed the firm globes of his lover's ass. "Or this." He kissed down Dean's chest. "I could map out every inch of you."

Dean moaned loudly. "All of the above, please."

"As you wish."

Chapter Twenty-Six

Dean woke up Christmas morning, actually excited about the holiday. It was his first official Christmas with Ryder. Last year, with Ryder overseas and him being too depressed about losing Dax, it hadn't been a good one. But he just knew today would be. He reached over, surprised to feel cool sheets instead of warm skin.

Sitting up, he saw that Ryder wasn't in the bedroom. He slipped on a T-shirt and padded downstairs. He stopped as he saw the lounge, stunned. Ryder had a tray of cinnamon buns and coffee on the table next to a roaring fire. But there was now a small Christmas tree and presents underneath that hadn't been there the night before. There was also tinsel and paper snowflakes. When he glanced up, he saw mistletoe.

"Ry?"

Ryder turned from where he was kneeling by the tree, arranging the gifts. He gave Dean a rare shy smile. "Surprise!" He stood slowly. "Do you like it?"

With a big grin, Dean said, "Babe, when did you have time to do all this?"

"It didn't take long." Ryder walked over to him. He still had bedhead, and he was wearing sweats and his Army T-shirt. Dean thought about unwrapping him—he was all he wanted this Christmas.

"Where did you get the tree?"

"Set it up with the resort who delivered it." Ryder kissed him. "Mistletoe."

Dean cupped the back of Ryder's head and pulled him in for a longer, slow kiss. "I love it. Almost as much as I love you."

Ryder's eyes lit up as he took Dean's hand. They moved to the blanket and pillows spread out by the fireplace. Ryder got their breakfast and they shared a warm, gooey and delicious cinnamon roll and sipped coffee.

"You told me you love Christmas," Ryder said, "I wanted to do something special, since I now have a reason to start loving it too."

After wrapping an arm around Ryder, Dean curled into his lover's side. "When I was a kid for a while I didn't get the fuss about it. You know my parents. They'd give me a new Bible and sweaters and that was that. Extra church, lots of nativity stuff. But then, when I was seven, I spent the night with Dax, and Beth—she goes the whole nine yards, yanno?" Dean recalled happily. "There was a big tree, tons of gifts. Dax's dad pretended to be Santa. It was awesome. Every year they included me after that. Dax, he loved Christmas like his dad." Dax had followed in his dad's footsteps and joined the Army. And just like his dad, one Christmas he didn't come home. Dean shook away the morose thoughts that would only make him sad. Better to focus on the here and now. Ryder was here, this was their first of hopefully many happy Christmases. Dax would be happy to see him enjoying the holiday again.

"I never really got to celebrate it much," Ryder admitted. "I was usually at the group home around the time and we got handouts and knockoffs." He shrugged. "I always thought to myself that when I got my own family, we'd have huge Christmases. Go all out." He played with his coffee cup. "I can see it. Our kids coming down like you did, presents covering the floor. Decorations everywhere, a tree that touches the ceiling, and even you as Santa."

Heart skipping a beat at the scene Ryder had painted, Dean could see it too. And he was thrilled that Ryder was seeing a future like that for them. Good to know they were on the same page. Made him think it was time to start looking for a ring. "I can see that too." He twined their fingers together.

"Though you might be a better Santa."

Ryder chuckled. "We could take turns."

"That works." Dean stole a kiss. "When the time comes, we can do all of that and anything else you want. Our kids are going to be spoiled, but they're going to know how loved they are, too."

"Yeah, exactly," Ryder agreed. He bit his lip. "So, not too soon to talk about this then?"

"No, we both want kids. Someday. Someday soon." He locked gazes with Ryder. "Of course, I'd like to put a ring on your finger first."

Ryder's face split into a grin. "Not if I beat you to it."

That got Dean curious—was he already planning something? A thought occurred, maybe he should propose after Ryder got his medal. Get down on one knee in front of everyone after the ceremony, show them all that this brave hero was his. His alone. And he wanted him for the rest of his life. "Oh really?" he managed to say before Ryder kissed him to distraction.

"Yep," Ryder said, then passed him a present. "Merry Christmas, Dean. Not a ring, not yet. But hopefully you like it."

Dean decided that when they got home he was going to start looking for rings. Maybe Beth and Jessie could help him with his plan. He took the gift. With his free hand, he cupped Ryder's cheek. "Merry Christmas, Ry. I've already gotten what I wanted but I can't wait to see what this is."

"Oh?" Ryder leaned into the touch.

"You." It was Christmas, he could be a little sappy, right? He knew fate could've easily taken a different turn and left him lonely and heartbroken but instead had given him a gift.

As he broke into a smile that lit up his whole face, Ryder said, "I love you."

"I love you, too." Dean carefully unwrapped the gift. It was thin and light. Tearing away the paper revealed a folder, which he opened, then gasped. Ryder had drawn a cover for his book, Crossroads. He hadn't shown it to anyone else but Ryder—it was a rough draft of a young adult story based on the truth of his teenage years. He wanted to let others know that they weren't alone and it really did get better. He traced his fingers over the sketch, done in vivid colors with colored pencils. A boy, stood at the crossroads. Darkness behind and light ahead. Ryder had beautifully depicted the tone and character. It was better than he could've imagined the cover being. "Wow. Just wow."

"Your story is incredible, baby. I know you're nervous about getting it published but I believe in you and I just had to draw this after reading it." Ryder bit his lip. "Do you like it?"

"It's perfect." Dean tore his eyes away from the cover art to lock on Ryder. "Seriously, it's exactly what I had in mind but better. I love it." He leaned over for a kiss. "Thank you. I think when we get home I'll look into publishers."

"You're welcome. Anyone would be crazy if they didn't say yes."

Dean felt his cheeks redden. "Flattery will get you everywhere."

"Not flattery, truth," Ryder corrected. "You've got a hell of a story written."

"And now an amazing cover." Dean's gaze returned to the sketch. "You could do this professionally."

"Nah, I'd rather design buildings." Ryder paused. "I only made an exception for you."

"Lucky me." Dean smiled then reached over to hand Ryder his present. "Your turn."

"You didn't have to get me anything. You got me the board. I don't even wanna know how much that cost you."

"Doesn't matter, it was worth it to see you so happy."

With a tender look, Ryder said, "You're spoiling me."

"You deserve it." Dean smiled softly. "Go on, open it."

Ryder took the present and quickly tore the wrapping from a necklace case. He stared at it for a moment and Dean hoped he'd gotten it right. He'd wanted to do something special and when the idea had come to him, he'd thought that couple's dog tags were perfect. Ryder's eyes widened as he popped open the case and saw them. He picked one up—it had his name and birth date and on the back—*Keep me close to your heart.*

The other necklace had Ryder's name and birth date. And the back had the same inscription. Ryder passed him that one then slipped his around his neck.

"I thought if you want you could put it on the same chain as your tags," Dean suggested. "If you want."

"I think I'll put my tags on this one." Ryder grinned, eyes a bit misty. "Thank you, baby. This is such a great idea." He helped Dean with his then kissed him deeply. "Always close to my heart."

"Always," Dean whispered back, climbing into Ryder's lap. It was time to unwrap his present and show Ryder how much he loved celebrating this Christmas with him.

Chapter Twenty-Seven

The day they got home, Dean called Jessie. "Hey, Jess. We're home. Do you want to meet for coffee and I'll treat you for taking care of my little monster?"

She giggled. "She wasn't that bad but she has been clingy. How about Starbucks?"

"That'll work, I wanted to talk to you about something."

"I've got news, too."

"Oh?" He was curious and hoped she had something good to tell him.

"Mm, I'll tell you when I see you." She paused. "Sassy, down! Okay, I'm going to leave, I think she knows who I'm talking to."

Dean laughed. "Of course she does. See you in a few."

Ryder had made a trip to campus for textbooks so Dean jogged to Starbucks. Jessie arrived a few minutes later. He ordered their coffees and they found a table outside as Sassy couldn't go inside. His dog was overjoyed to see him—she ran from Jessie, jumped into his lap, and refused to budge. He petted her as she licked his hand and snuggled closer for warmth. He tucked her in his jacket and she nestled her head on his chest, her big brown eyes watching him. He'd missed his little diva. He rubbed her ears and knew he'd need a few treats to make up for leaving her.

"So, you look like you had an amazing vacation," Jessie teased, reaching over to tug on his scarf, which was hiding a love bite that was just a little above the collar.

He chuckled. "Definitely amazing. I wish we could've stayed longer. It was just what Ry and I needed."

"I'm glad." Jesse smiled. "So, what did you want to talk

about?"

"You first." Dean took a sip of his coffee. "You sounded nervous. Is everything okay?"

"Yeah." Jesse absently played with the sleeve on her cup. "It's good, actually. Well, I hope so." She brushed her hair back behind her ear. "I, uh, I have a date Friday."

That surprised Dean. "With who?"

"His name is Scott. We met in grief counseling. He lost his wife three years ago in a car accident. Anyway, he's nice. He gets how I feel. We've been talking and he asked me to dinner."

"That's good." Dean reached over and took her hand to stop her fidgeting. "Jess, it's okay. It's been over a year, sweetie."

Tears filled her eyes. "I know, but it doesn't hurt any less."

"You're right about that," he agreed. "But it's good you have Scott to talk to. Ryder's helped me so much."

"But you don't have to feel like you're betraying him," Jesse whispered. "I do. Like if I move on, I'm giving up on this crazy hope that it's all a bad dream and he'll come home."

Dean couldn't speak. Not without crying as he saw the anguish on Jessie's face. Still holding Sassy, he managed to slide over to the seat next to Jessie and wrapped his other arm around her. She sniffled into his chest. He knew they were getting curious stares but ignored them. He managed to say, "You're not betraying Dax. He wouldn't want you to be this miserable and lonely."

"Then he shouldn't have left me!" Jessie cried. Sassy whined and seeming to sense Jessie's need for comfort she moved over to Jessie's lap to cuddle. Jessie hugged Sassy, stroking her fur.

Dean could understand her upset. Losing Dax had been the worst thing to ever happen to him. He'd been angry too. Hurt. And lost. He'd only healed because of Ryder. And losing him? Dean couldn't even imagine it. In Jessie's shoes, he probably couldn't even get out of bed every day. She'd been so strong, through it all. He had to help her now. "Shh, I know you're angry. It is unfair, Jess. I wish more than anything he was still with us. But he's gone. And yeah, it hurts so bad. But we're still here and the best thing we can do to honor his sacrifice is be happy like he wanted and make the most of every day. I'm here if you need me, just remember that. I get it, and I'll help you through it."

"Thanks, Dean." Jessie hugged him tightly. "I do need help, that's why I've been going to counseling. I guess it's bringing up a lot of stuff. Going through the stages, y'know? You're right about everything, it's just so hard to let go."

"Because you had a real love with Dax. That won't ever go away, but that's not necessarily a bad thing. You two had something special."

"We did. And I'll never forget he loved me with all he had." She pulled back and swiped at her eyes. "I'm lucky to have had that. I just thought he was the one. I guess I wonder if I'll ever find love like that again."

"You won't find what you had with him, but I believe in love. You'll find someone, something special in a different way." Dean handed her a napkin to wipe her tears. "Give Scott a chance. You'll never know if you don't try."

Jessie nodded. "You're not upset then that I said yes?"

"No, of course not." Dean smiled at her in reassurance. He knew what she was thinking, but she had to move on. It wasn't like she and Dax had willingly separated. If he was still alive, they'd be together. He knew that and didn't hold it against her that she was contemplating dating again. He only hoped that Scott treated her right, or he'd have to answer to him. He'd look out for Jessie, Dax would want that. And he loved her like a sister. "You're family to me, Jess. I want you happy and smiling again. You deserve that."

"I love you, Dean." Jessie hugged him again.

He kissed her temple. "Right back at you." He paused. "Just know he'll answer to me if he ever hurts you. And then Ryder who will be right behind me." Sassy barked and they both laughed. "And Sassy too apparently."

Jessie chuckled. "You'll all be too late, as Daddy will be cleaning his gun Friday." She shook her head. "No scaring him off, so no, I haven't told him how protective everyone is, but I think he knows."

Laughing with her, Dean said, "Good. You'll have to call me and tell me how it goes."

"I will," she promised. She reached for her coffee. "Okay, now that I've caused a spectacle, what did you want to tell me?"

Deciding that now wasn't a good time to bring it up, not after the conversation they had just had, Dean instead said, "I'm looking into getting my book published."

Jessie smiled. "Awesome!"

"Yeah, Ry drew a stunning cover for it and convinced me I should."

"That's great." Jessie stared at him for a minute. "Not what you were going to tell me, though, is it?"

Dean shrugged. "It can wait."

She swatted his arm and Sassy growled. Dean scooped his dog up and chided her for it, but Sassy just wagged her tail and played cute. He rolled his eyes and Jessie shook her head. "Silly dog, did you forget I took care of you all week?" Sassy tilted her head, staring at Jessie, then she barked and burrowed into Dean's jacket. Sassy was a little handful, but he loved her and she knew it.

"Now, back to what I was going to say," Jessie steered back to the topic. "It can't wait. You were over the moon when you walked in. Don't worry about upsetting me, I've cried all I can today."

Should he tell her? Maybe it would cheer her up. Hopefully it wouldn't make her sadder. He didn't want to rub it in. He hadn't even thought of that until now. How he was thinking of marrying Ryder and she had lost the chance to with Dax. He felt like a jerk. He had just been so excited that he hadn't thought it through. He'd just wanted to share the news with his closest friend and, like he said, family. Deep down, he knew she'd be thrilled. And like he had told her, Dax would want them to make the most of things and find their happiness. Ryder was his. He cleared his throat. "I want to ask Ry to marry me," he confessed.

Jessie let out a cry of delight and clapped. "Yes! Oh my God, when are you going to ask?"

So, Dean told her his plans. "We could get married there, at the courthouse, then have a small reception when we get home."

"Leave the reception to me. I'll get Beth to help," Jessie offered.

"Really? You wouldn't mind?"

"No, I'd love to do that for you guys." Jessie smiled brightly. "Can I tag along? I want to be there when you ask. He's going to be so surprised!"

"I hope so. You think it's a good idea?"

"Yes! It's so sweet and romantic."

Dean grinned. "Well then, let's get to planning."

Chapter Twenty-Eight

A week later, Dean had picked out a ring and after getting it from the jewelry store, he headed home. Then he had to figure out where to hide it so Ryder didn't accidently find it before it was time. He decided to stash it in the spare bedroom. Opening the closet, he saw Ryder's old duffle bag and, bypassing it, he reached up to pull down a box of books. He put the tiny ring box under his collection of Wilde just as the front door opened. Sassy, who was lounging on the guest bed, wagged her tail and barked.

"Go distract him, Sassy," Dean said and their dog ran off. He grabbed a paperback, an excuse as to why he was rummaging, then he tucked the box back up on a shelf. He walked out to the front room, where Ryder was playing fetch with a small ball as Sassy bounced around.

"Hey, babe," Dean greeted with a kiss.

"Hey, baby." Ryder tugged him into an embrace and deepened the kiss. "Whatcha got there?"

"Oh, I was searching for some of my Sherlock books. Some of my students are interested in reading them."

Ryder glanced at the book. "*Hound of the Baskervilles*. That's a good one."

With a nod, Dean decided to change the subject before he blurted out what he was actually doing. He didn't like keeping anything from Ryder but he wanted him to be surprised. "How was class?"

"Good. I think I did well on the test. I hope I did anyway."

"I'm sure you did." Dean cupped the back of Ryder's neck and played with the curls there.

"I did have an excellent tutor." Ryder grinned.

Dean blushed slightly. "You already thanked me for that... Twice."

"Hmm, I was really grateful." Ryder ran a hand down Dean's back. "We staying in tonight?"

Dean wanted to drag Ryder to bed and spend the night there. But then he remembered his earlier conversation with Michael. And how much fun he and Ryder could have on the dance floor. "Actually, Mike and Jules invited us to go out for drinks tonight at the bar. Maybe we could even do some dancing." He swayed slightly as he wrapped his arms around Ryder's neck.

"That sounds like a good time." Ryder brushed their lips together. "You gonna wear those jeans with the hole in the knee?"

"Only if you wear those tight black ones." Dean was getting excited just thinking about it—Ryder was sex on legs in them. Not that he wasn't already, but damn, he liked showing him off then taking him home to peel them off him.

With a smirk, Ryder squeezed his ass. "Lost in thought there, baby?"

Rubbing against Ryder's thigh, he let his lover know just what he was thinking. Though it was obvious, judging by the similar bulge in Ryder's pants. "Mm, I don't see us sleeping much later."

"I'm good with that." Ryder dipped his hand into his jeans. "Not sure I want to wait until later, though. When are we supposed to meet them?"

He kissed along Ryder's jaw. "We have time if we shower together."

Ryder's cell rang from his back pocket and they both groaned. "Let me just shut it off." He pulled it out and glanced at the number. "It's Joel."

"See if he and Lucy can join us," Dean suggested, bending his head a little so he could kiss and suck on Ryder's neck. The slight scruff scratched his cheeks and aroused him some more.

Ryder answered the call, "Hey, Joel. I'm kinda busy, what's up?"

"Kinda busy?" Dean breathed. *I'll just have to try harder.* He cupped Ryder through the denim and saw Ryder bite his lip. Dean smirked then pouted as Ryder stepped back. Ryder kissed his palm and suddenly seemed concerned by whatever Joel was saying. "Oh, man, I'm sorry. Of course... Let me just ask Dean..."

The fog of desire lifted and a little of his need subsided. What was wrong? He was having such a good day. "Lucy's mom was in a minor car wreck. They need to go to Fayetteville, but don't want to drag Amelia along. They wanted to know if we could watch her for a couple of hours?"

"Yeah, tell Joel to bring her over." Dean pecked his partner's lips then went around straightening up the house as Ryder finished the call. He grabbed his phone from the counter and texted Michael and Jules to let them know that they couldn't make it as a friend had an emergency. He was still getting used to his two closest friends being together but he was happy for them. He didn't know all the details as the relationship was new, but they seemed good for one another. Michael had settled down a bit, and Jules seemed happier than he'd been in a while.

"I'm so sorry," Ryder said after he hung up. "I was looking forward to our date night."

"Me too. We'll do it tomorrow or the next night," Dean replied, placing his cell down. "This was important."

"Yeah, of course and I'm glad we could help them out." Ryder rubbed the back of his neck. "You ready for a ten-month-old? I've never cared for a baby."

"We'll figure it out. Don't worry." Dean took Ryder's hand and tugged him over to the couch. They sat down and Dean leaned in for another kiss. "I know we can't do anything — not enough time. But this —"

"This we can do," Ryder agreed, his lips meeting Dean's again.

* * * *

About fifteen minutes later there was a knock on the door. They broke apart from their heated make-out session and composed themselves. Dean scooped Sassy up and quickly put her in the bedroom before joining Ryder at the door. He waited for Dean then pulled it open.

"Hey, Lucy, we're sorry about your mom," Ryder said. "She's going to be okay?"

"Yeah, just a fractured wrist and some bruises," Lucy told them, seeming on the verge of tears. "I just want to make sure she's all right, y'know?"

"Of course," Dean said.

"Thank you so much." Lucy gave them both a hug. "Our babysitter is visiting family and so Joel thought to ask you. I didn't want to impose but I don't want Amelia going to the hospital either."

"It's no trouble," Ryder assured. "You're like family to us. We're always here when you need us."

Dean took Amelia from Lucy and the little girl rested her head on his shoulder, cuddling close. "And you don't have to worry about rushing back. If you need to stay just call."

"Really?" Lucy seemed relieved. "We brought her playpen just in case. Joel's getting it now."

"Let me go help," Ryder offered. "So you can get there before visiting hours are over."

"I owe you both." Lucy kissed Amelia's temple. "You be good, sweetpea. Mommy and Daddy will be back soon. Uncle Ryder and Uncle Dean are going to take good care of you."

Dean was touched that Lucy had made him an honorary uncle. He rubbed Amelia's back as she fussed. He wanted to tell her about his planned proposal, but now wasn't the time. Instead, he looked at Amelia. "We're going to have fun. Don't worry. Anything I need to know?"

"Her dinner is packed, she usually eats around five. She likes a bottle and story before bed. Bedtime is at eight. Once you lay her down, try not to pick her up unless she's overly upset. She's should just fall right to sleep, though." Lucy smiled. "That's all I can think of. Oh! Her Pooh bear—she has to have him to sleep."

Dean returned the smile. "Got it."

Ryder returned, carrying the playpen, and Joel had a diaper bag and cooler he set inside. Ryder gave Joel a fist bump, Joel hugged Amelia then Lucy did too, and after thanking Dean and Ryder again they left.

"Where should we set up the playpen?"

"Well, if she does stay tonight, maybe our room? We don't have baby monitors and I want to be able to hear her."

"Good thinking."

"Let's set up her play mat and give her some toys for now."

Ryder grabbed the diaper bag. Dean carried Amelia to the front room where they set everything up. He sat Amelia on the mat and they found a barnyard animal set that she began to play with.

After letting Sassy out, Ryder joined Dean on the floor and they watched Amelia. Sassy gave the little girl a kiss then wandered off. Amelia picked up a cow and moved it from one hand to the other. Dean took the pig and started telling her what it was and what sound it made. He did the same for the horse and cow with Amelia giggling and taking the toys from him. She was the cutest baby—big brown eyes and curly black hair. And Lucy had her dressed in a lavender dress with a matching bow and socks.

"You're amazing with her," Ryder said quietly when Amelia crawled over and climbed into Dean's lap. He started playing patty-cake and again she laughed. "I'm kinda nervous to even pick her up."

"It's easy. Here, babe." Dean took one of Amelia's books from the bag and gave it to Ryder. He then moved Amelia over to his lap. She patted the star on the cover and gave Ryder a doe-eyed look.

"Oh, man, we're so going to spoil her and buy her

anything she wants with that look."

Laughing, Dean just shook his head. "Right? She has us both wrapped around her little finger."

"Definitely." Ryder opened the book and read her the tale of the baby star. Dean snatched his phone and got a picture of them. It was too adorable not to. Amelia was staring at the pages as Ryder's soft voice brought the story to life. And Ryder thought he was amazing?

With a grin, Dean pictured a few years down the road. Married with kids of their own. Content to spend a night in like this, just being a family. He wanted that, so much. He leaned over and kissed Ryder when he was finished reading.

"Are you thinking about what I think you are?"

"Yeah, couldn't help it," Dean admitted. They'd already talked about having kids someday so he knew that Ryder was probably thinking the same right about now.

"So we didn't talk about this yet. Adoption or surrogacy?" Ryder asked. "Not now, of course. I mean when we're ready. After I've got a job and—"

Dean pressed a finger to his lips. "I know, Ry. Maybe both? I'd like to have a child of our own but I'd like to be foster parents too." He knew this was the right answer when Ryder's face lit up.

"Yeah," Ryder agreed, giving Amelia another toy. "I want that, too. I've always wanted to adopt, give a kid, like I was, a real home. A place to belong, family to love them..."

Dean nodded. He had been lucky to have Beth and Dax. He wished Ryder had been too. Instead of going through all the foster homes and not having a family. "You never told me. How many foster homes did you go to?"

"Eight, I think. I kinda lost count." Ryder shrugged.

Dean sighed as he scooted closer to Ryder. He wanted to make all of that past hurt go away. Maybe he should just let it drop. But then it might be good for Ryder to talk. They'd both helped one another to let the past go and were starting a future. He put his arm around him as Amelia crawled off his lap and started to explore the area with Sassy now following along. "And none of them worked?"

"There was one time, almost. I learned after that to never get my hopes up."

"What happened?"

Ryder rested his head on Dean's shoulder. "I was seven, maybe? They were a nice couple. Bought me new shoes, actually gave me a birthday cake... Said they wanted to adopt. And then they found out they were expecting. I couldn't compete with a new baby. They made excuses and sent me packing."

"That's awful." Dean kissed the top of Ryder's head.

"Not the worst that ever happened." Ryder took his hand. "I just want us to help at least one kid avoid that."

"We will," Dean promised, twining their fingers together. They laughed as Sassy nudged Amelia back toward her play mat. "You know too, Ry, you helped Amelia. She'll thank you one day for what you did."

Ryder nodded. "I don't know how I didn't see before the good that came out of what I did. But I do now."

"I'm glad." Dean squeezed his hand.

They fell silent for a few minutes. Then Ryder spoke, "Dean... If we do have a baby and it's a boy, I'd like to have Dax be his middle name."

Dean couldn't speak for a moment, floored by Ryder's words. He thought of Dax, the family and gang of kids he'd wanted, and how he'd asked for him to be happy and do everything he couldn't. He definitely wanted to honor his brother and was touched that Ryder did too. "I'd like that..."

"I think he kind of brought us together."

"Yeah, he did," Dean managed to say, swallowing the lump in his throat. "Before you got hurt I asked him to look out for you and make sure you got home. I'm not much for praying or believing, but I think he was watching over us."

"I think so, too. I wish I could've met him," Ryder admitted. "Thank him for what he did, all he did. Not just his duty either, but all he did for you."

"Me too." Dean hugged him. "He'd have liked you, I know it." He remembered when Dax had asked Jessie to marry him, he'd been surprised it'd happened so fast. Dax'd told Dean that one day he would get it. That surrounded by love and family, he had been right where he belonged. And Dax had intended to make the most of that. He'd been right. Dean did get it now and as he often did he followed his brother's advice. *"When you find him, Dean, when you know, hold on. Hold on and make sure he knows, like I made sure Jessie did, that you need him like you need to breathe. A love like that, it ain't easy to find but you will. I'll make sure of it. Just like you helped Jessie see I was more than just a stubborn idiot if she only gave me a chance."*

Smiling at the memory, Dean held onto Ryder a little tighter. Silently, he thanked Dax for keeping his promise.

* * * *

Ryder rocked Amelia, walking back and forth across the room as he lulled her to sleep. He'd been worried at first about dropping her, tripping, but as soon as Dean had sat her in his lap, he knew he'd never let anything happen to her. She clutched her bear and had one tiny hand tangled in his shirt. She had bawled when they put her to bed and neither he nor Dean could stand to see her cry. His partner was now ordering pizza while he hoped to get her to calm down. She had her eyes nearly closed, almost out.

He smiled at her. He had meant what he'd told Dean earlier—he saw the good he'd done every time he looked at Amelia. He still didn't think he deserved a medal—just knowing Joel was alive and here for his family was enough. He'd do it all again. And that was because of Dean. He knew Dean would catch him every time he fell.

It wouldn't be long now before he could finally pop the question. He'd already practiced getting down on one knee a few times. He wanted it to be perfect. To show Dean how much he loved him. How lucky he was to be able to dream. To hope. He'd never allowed himself that before now. Too risky, too much fear of being hurt. But not anymore. He was right where he belonged. And he could dream of a family, a future with a man who had saved him. Funny how it'd all started with a few letters. It had been fate, he believed that.

"Babe," Dean said quietly from the doorway. He loved it when he called him that, drove him a good kinda crazy. "She asleep?"

"I think so." Ryder carried Amelia over to the playpen. Dean helped him lay her down, then they tucked a blanket around her, kissing her temple before turning out the light. They paused at the door, but not hearing a peep, they left the room.

Dean smiled. "Pizza will be here soon. I got Netflix ready."

Ryder had noticed he had been in a really good mood and wondered what was going on. Had he found the ring in his duffle bag? He hoped not, he wanted to surprise him. Then again, maybe Dean himself had something planned. He didn't doubt that his lover wanted the commitment as much as he did. They'd both hinted at it. If Dean proposed before the ceremony then he'd just change things slightly. Either way, no matter what happened he was marrying Dean before they left Washington. He was going to put a ring on his finger and love him for the rest of his life. He knew just what he wanted. It was right here in front of him.

He tugged Dean close and brushed their lips together. "Perfect."

Chapter Twenty-Nine

Two months later

Ryder was surprisingly calm while meeting the President. He stood proudly at the podium, in his mess dress. He could see Dean, Beth and Jessie in the second row. Dean was dressed in an Armani suit with a tie that matched the color of Ryder's jacket. He was stunningly gorgeous, Ryder thought.

His men were there as well, including Joel's family. Except for Bentley, of course, as he was currently doing jail time. A bunch of reporters, some Congressmen and other Army personnel were seated as well. It seemed like a lot of fuss for him. At the same time, he was incredibly proud. He had served his country with honor, given above and beyond as the President was saying, and he had gotten his men home. Losing his leg had been a hell of a sacrifice but he'd go through it all again to end up here, about to propose to Dean. The ring box was in his pocket and that made him nervous.

Dean smiled at him. That *smile* that was for him alone. He met Dean's gaze and the tension in him eased. Dean would be his fiancé before the night was over. He had no doubt that his lover would say yes. He simply had to find the right moment.

He listened as the President recounted the nightmare of that day. Joel hadn't lost his sight, he had healed completely. And his other men hadn't gotten a scratch on them.

As the President talked about his injury and recovery, Ryder realized there was one thing he'd change if he could.

He would've called Dean that first day in the hospital. He'd have come to Germany if asked. He'd have stopped the depression before it had gotten so bad. Ryder counted his lucky stars that Dean had come to the hospital even after receiving that stupid note of his.

The President, of course, left out the details of Bentley and the hell he'd caused. Despite that, though, and a few other bumps, it had been a good eight months. Best time of his life really. He was getting a degree with his GI benefits, he had created a home with Dean, gained a family, and fallen hard for a shy English teacher who he intended to spend the rest of his life with.

The ceremony continued and before long the Medal of Honor was placed around his neck. The five pointed gold star was surrounded by a laurel wreath, suspended from a gold bar with 'Valor' inscribed and surmounted by an eagle. Minerva's head was in the center of the star surrounded by the words, United States of America.

"Thank you, Mr. President." Ryder saluted.

"Your country and I thank you for your service and heroism, Sergeant Brooks."

* * * *

After the ceremony, Ryder was interviewed. Dean stood to the side, watching as Ryder fidgeted and bit his lip as he answered questions. He was honored, but he didn't like all the attention on him. Dean could see the reporters loved him, though, and his modesty as he said he'd only wanted to keep all his men safe and bring them home, no matter the cost. He was genuine and Dean couldn't be more proud to be his partner. Then there was a banquet held. Before they took their seats, Beth and Jessie both insisted on pictures of him and Ryder together. He and Ryder indulged them— arms wrapped around each other, they posed for the camera.

"I'm so proud of you, Ry," Dean said, briefly squeezing

his hand. He boldly leaned in and kissed his cheek. "So proud."

"Thanks." Ryder grinned. "Dean, there's, uh, something I want to ask you."

"You know you can ask me anything." Dean was confused then it hit him. Was Ryder going to propose? "Oh my God, Ry! I was going to ask you something."

Ryder raised his eyebrows then he seemed to realize what was going on. His eyes widened. "Really?"

With a nod, Dean pulled out the ring box from his pocket and Ryder did the same. "You know great minds think alike."

"I just… This is a big moment but I wouldn't be here if it wasn't for you, baby," Ryder said quietly. Dean could see that they had a few people's attention now but he didn't care. He was focused solely on Ryder. He was awed that they both had planned to make this day so special.

"How about we ask each other?" Dean took his hand. "You first."

People gathered around them. His mama already had tears in her eyes and Jessie was smiling.

Ryder cleared his throat. "Your letters from home, they gave me courage, strength, and hope. I found myself falling for you before I even met you. And then I lost my leg and suffered PTSD. I was ready to give up, because I thought I had lost my chance with you. Then you came into the hospital and showed me that life was just beginning. At that moment, I knew I never wanted to let you go. Not ever. You helped me heal, you got me on track, and gave me what I needed most. I love you, Dean. I want to be with you, just you, for the rest of my life." Ryder paused and smoothly got down on one knee. He popped open his ring box. "Dean Anders, will you please marry me?"

"Yes!" Dean knew he was grinning from ear to ear. "Of course I will!" He blinked away the moisture in his eyes and held out his hand. Ryder slipped a silver band on his ring finger then Dean helped him to his feet and pecked him on the lips. There was a cheer and some *awws* as they hugged tightly.

"Your turn," Ryder said when they pulled back.

Dean took a moment to compose himself. "I didn't know it at the time but deciding to become a pen pal was one of the best decisions I've ever made. I found my best friend. I fell in love with you before I even realized it. When we met you were in a bad way, but I was determined to get you to see that you were still perfect to me. I knew I was so lucky to still have you, to have not lost you... Every time I see you, I think of the gift I've been given. The love you've given me, the hope. And I've never been happier. All I want is for our love to keeping growing as we spend the rest of our lives together." He paused. "I love you, Ry, More than life." He dropped to one knee and opened his little box. "Will you please marry me, Sergeant Ryder Brooks?"

"Yes!" Ryder let him slip the ring on then Dean stood. To his surprise, Ryder kissed him tenderly. "Yes, a thousand times."

He was still smiling. There was applause all around them. Ryder put his arm around Dean and tugged him close. "When's the wedding?" a reporter asked.

"We're going to the courthouse tomorrow," they said in unison, then they both laughed.

Dean shared a look with Ryder. "Really? You planned it too?"

"Yep, and we're staying in the honeymoon suite," Ryder said with a grin. "I didn't want to wait."

"Me either."

Beth and Jessie both hugged them. "I'm so happy for you boys!" Beth gushed. "And Jessie and I have a reception planned when you get back."

"You knew Ryder was going to ask," Dean said.

"He wanted my blessing. I gave it to him, of course. And then you told me your plans so I just made sure they both went together while keeping it a surprise."

"Thanks, Mama." Dean hugged her again. "I wish Dax

was here."

"He is, in spirit." His mama smiled. "I know that."

"Yeah, he is," Jessie agreed.

Dean believed it too. And he knew how happy his brother would've been. They were interviewed and asked about the proposal. "I told Ryder once that if I could I'd shout my love for him to everyone. This seemed like a good place to do that. He's my hero, and I'm so lucky to have him."

Ryder kissed his temple. "No, that'd be me."

Epilogue

Lying in bed, tangled together among the rumpled sheets, Dean was snuggled into Ryder's side. He had his head lying on Ryder's shoulder and he was idly tracing the ring on Ryder's finger. They were married. He was now Dean Anders-Brooks. And he couldn't wipe the huge grin off his face as he thought about the proposal and the commitment they'd made to one another in the courthouse earlier that day.

Ryder kissed the top of his head then took his hand, lining up their rings. He too had a smile that lit up his face. "God, I love you."

He tilted his head up to meet Ryder's gaze. He leaned in for a soft kiss. "I love you, Mr. Anders-Brooks."

Ryder chuckled. "That's got a nice ring to it."

Propping himself up on Ryder's chest, Dean asked, "I'm curious, when did you pick out the ring?"

"Ah..." Ryder ran his hand down Dean's back. "It was actually the day Bentley came after you. Part of the reason I had that meltdown," he admitted.

Things about that day now made a little more sense. He could just imagine how Ryder had felt, being so happy then having that joy crushed. But they'd gotten through it together, and he'd proven to Ryder that he wasn't going anywhere. Not ever. He caressed Ryder's cheek, brushing their lips together. "You know, if you had asked me that night I'd have said yes in a heartbeat."

"Yeah, I do." Ryder's smile returned. "It was so hard

these past few months not to ask you. I wanted to so bad, especially at Christmas."

"That's when I came up with the idea to propose at the ceremony," Dean told him. "I could see our future so clearly and I just wanted our dreams to come true."

Ryder ran his fingers through Dean's tangled hair. "They have and you'd better think up some new ones 'cause I'm going to make those come true, too."

Kids. White picket fence. They already had the dog. A happily ever after, the kind that didn't happen often enough, but he'd gotten it. And he couldn't be happier. He had Ryder forever and all he wanted was to make love to him, lose himself in this beautiful moment and the man who was his whole world. "'Kay, but for now, just keep those kisses coming."

Ryder rolled them so that he was on top then drew Dean in for a long, slow kiss. "Like this?" he breathed. He kissed along Dean's jaw. "So gorgeous, and all mine."

"Always," Dean promised, twining their hands together.

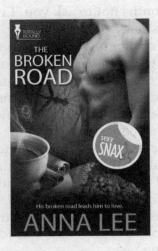

The Broken Road

Excerpt

Chapter One

Kason knew he was going to have to stop this before he was caught. Going to The Daily Grind every morning for the past week and staying for hours on end had to have been noticed by the staff and the owner, Ryen Moore. Ryen was his problem—or maybe not a problem per se, but his reason for sticking around. He'd met Ryen after coming into the coffee shop on a whim to wait for his sister, Lexie, and had felt an instant attraction to him. Ryen was his type, and perfect, from what he'd learned while sitting there pretending to drink the coffee he normally avoided because it made him jittery.

Handsome and charming, Ryen had coffee-brown eyes and a mop of black hair that flopped adorably over them, causing him to brush it back whenever he was irritated. Today he was wearing a Ralph Lauren polo shirt and faded blue jeans. He was tall and strong, with muscular forearms that made Kason think of how easily Ryen could make him forget all about his problems for a while.

"How's the blueberry muffin today?"

"Oh, um, it was…really good…" Kason passed Ryen the plate with the remaining crumbs.

"Good. Need anything?" Ryen often talked to him about everyday things—the weather, the coffee, interests they shared—but nothing too personal, as if he was hesitant or maybe just bothered by Kason practically stalking him here.

Kason could think of a few things he wanted from Ryen. He didn't have the courage to ask if he would sit and talk over coffee. Besides, Ryen wouldn't be interested. No one was anymore.

"No, thanks." He forced a smile.

Ryen seemed concerned, but then another customer gestured for him and he had to leave. With a sigh, Kason stared at his laptop. Why was he putting himself through this?

He knew why. He wanted to ask Ryen out, to dinner, a movie or maybe a baseball game. He thought of it often. It was there on the tip of his tongue whenever Ryen spoke to him, yet he couldn't take the risk. Instead he sat there, laptop in front of him and an empty document, complete with blinking cursor, open. A cup of cold coffee by his left hand.

"I forgot to ask. Refill?" Ryen's deep voice cut through his thoughts and caused him to jerk his head up.

"Um, no thanks." Kason paused then gestured to the cup. "To be honest, more than one and I'm bouncing off the walls."

"So then, it's not the coffee, huh?" Ryen's gaze appeared to contain a hint of curiosity and that, combined with his words, left Kason confused.

"I'm sorry?"

"You know." Ryen put his hand on the table and leaned in a little. "You've been here every day this week. I know my coffee blends are good, but not that good."

"I...uh..." Kason tried not to get flustered as he met Ryen's gaze. That ended up being a mistake. The amusement there and the twinkle in his eyes had him wanting to pull Ryen closer. "I-I'm writing a screenplay, like I told you."

"Yeah, I remember. But what's it about?"

"Um, it's sci-fi. Aliens, time travel, you know, uh, that sort of stuff," he said lamely, wishing he could get his brain to work and stop him from babbling.

"Interesting." Ryen flashed him a bright smile, showing off his white teeth. He ducked his head around to peek at the screen. "You appear to be stuck."

"Yeah, writer's block." Kason knew his face was turning a bright red. He would've run out if he could.

"I see that." Ryen nodded. "So, tell me, how did you get to be so cute?"

More books from
Pride Publishing

In a shadowy game where defeat can mean death, a deal with the enemy can change things forever.

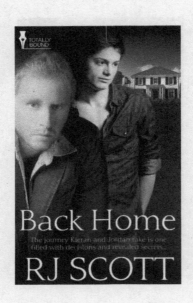

Kieran returns home to save his family. Can he do this without falling in love with Jordan again?

Seasons of Love follows forty years in the lives of two men.

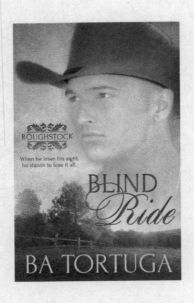

Jason Scott has everything a bull rider wants — but he stands to lose it all.

About the Author

Anna Lee

Anna Lee graduated from the University of California Riverside with a Bachelor's Degree in Creative Writing. Living with a disability, she has overcome many challenges and puts her passion for life and love into her writing. She lives with her family and dogs and enjoys writing late into the night. When she isn't writing Anna enjoys chasing after her nieces and nephew or chatting with her friends about her favorite books and TV shows.

Anna Lee loves to hear from readers. You can find contact information, website details and an author profile page at https://www.pride-publishing.com/